BREAKING TRAVIS

THE WEST SERIES

JILL SANDERS

GRAYTON

To all those bad boys,
who have a heart of pure gold

SUMMARY

Travis Nolan is back in town and doing everything he can to get right back out of it again. Finding out that his father devised a way to keep him locked in the small town of Fairplay, even after death, has him working overtime to complete his new obligations. But now there's a small pixy redhead that won't get out of his way or out of his mind.

Holly just wants to finish remodeling her business and apartment, so she can get the annoying Travis off her back but working closely with him has afforded her the opportunity to see what's behind his raw and rough exterior. And she's quickly losing her heart to the town's notorious bad boy.

*H*olly was going crazy. It had been two weeks since she'd shut down the old bookstore and moved. Two weeks of living in a strange place, in someone else's apartment. Two weeks of the daily stress of coordinating and working with all the contractors and laborers. Two weeks without working in her bookstore. But, other than a sore back from sleeping in a strange bed, she was loving every minute of it. She loved the hustle and bustle of construction. She enjoyed the sounds, the smells, and seeing the project moving forward each time she stepped inside the doors.

She couldn't stop herself from rushing down to the old brick building and seeing the work that was being done on it. Right now it didn't look much different than when the tornado had ripped through town over two years ago. But if you looked closely, you could see a method to the madness.

As she stood in the middle of the building she and her

mother had worked all their lives in, she couldn't help but smile. It was an early Sunday morning in late summer, and the place was quiet. She loved coming here when the workers weren't banging around and making loud noises. She could actually see the vision she and Mr. Nolan had painstakingly designed over several weeks.

Who knew that the mayor had an architecture background? Not her. When she had finally built up enough nerve to ask him about updating the building she leased from him, he'd not only jumped on board but had fronted the entire cost himself. Sure, the building was his and he could do whatever he wanted with it, but she never expected him to include her tiny apartment upstairs in the plans.

"Why not redo the whole place?" he'd suggested, walking around the downstairs that first day. "In the last two years, there have been more repairs on your apartment than down here. If we're going in for a penny, why not a pound and do it all at once."

She'd jumped at the chance, of course. He was right; her apartment was in dire need of updates. The roof leaked during heavy storms and some of the old wooden floorboards had come loose. She'd tried to cover them with rugs, but still, she stubbed her toes on them if she wasn't careful. The plumbing and electric for the entire building desperately needed to be replaced. She lost electricity a lot due to there not being enough volts going through the breaker box.

So, she and Mr. Nolan had gone down to the bank and signed an agreement that the town's lawyer, Grant Holton, who was also Holly's friend, had written up. The next week she started receiving bids on the construction and spent several days moving everything out of the two spaces, including herself.

She looked around and smiled. She didn't mind the mess or the hassles, especially since she knew what it would look like afterward. Her furniture and the bookstore's inventory were in storage, tucked away until when she could open Holly's, the first bookstore slash coffeehouse slash wine bar to grace the small town of Fairplay, Texas.

"Dreaming of what it will look like when it's done?" she heard behind her, causing her to jump a little.

"Oh!" She rested her hand over her heart. "Mr. Nolan, I didn't expect you here."

The older gentlemen stood in the doorway, his hands tucked into his pants. He looked tired. She'd known Roy Nolan all of her life. He'd been the town's mayor for as long as anyone could remember. He'd quietly stepped down when his wife of thirty plus years had gone nuts and tried to kill Grant. Then he'd retreated into his large white home just a few blocks from there. Their only child, Travis, had left town the same night they had hauled his mother away. Now she sat in a state mental hospital for the next twenty plus years. No one in town had heard from Travis since that night. It was rumored that Savannah Douglas had visited him on several occasions, but she didn't really talk to anyone about it.

"It looks a mess now, doesn't it, girlie?" he said, using his nickname for her as he walked into the empty room. All the walls were gone and the hardwood floor was completely ripped up, leaving only the cement floor.

"I can still see the potential." She turned and looked at him. "Especially with all the wonderful drawings you did." She smiled.

He nodded. "Well, girlie, you had a wonderful idea for this place. You know, I had big dreams for this town." He sighed and looked out the large front windows towards Main Street.

She walked over and rested her hand on his arm. They had talked about all of his plans for the small town. How he wanted to rebuild it, allow it to grow. "This is a wonderful first step."

He nodded. "I had hoped that…" He started and then shook his head.

"What?" She waited.

"I had hoped that Travis would come back and fall in love with this town. Everything I've worked so hard for…" He paused again, and Holly felt his arm stiffen. "Everything I did was for that boy."

She started to worry when he began shaking.

"Mr. Nolan? Are you alright?" She gripped his arm tighter, but he just looked off into the distance.

When he hunched forward and started to fall, she gripped his arm more tightly, trying to hold him upright, but the man's massive frame was too much for her tiny one. He hit the floor hard, causing her to land on her knees.

When she looked over, she saw that his face had gone completely white. Rushing over to him, she rolled him over onto his back and listened for a heartbeat. When she couldn't find one, she pulled her cell phone out of her purse and dialed 911.

"Hang on, Mr. Nolan, help is on the way," she reassured him, holding his hand in hers as tears slipped down her face.

CHAPTER 1

Travis stood stiffly in front of his old house with his hands clenched at this side. It was too dark to see anything clearly, especially since all the lights in the massive place were out. Too many memories flooded his mind. He wanted to escape them, but he knew he couldn't, not until his business was done and he could start fresh.

It had been almost a month since he'd gotten word that his father had passed away from a brain aneurysm. It had taken his father's lawyer almost two weeks to track him down in Montana. The fact that the lawyer was his ex-fiancée Alexis' husband, the man his mother had tried to murder, had just been the icing on the bitter cake he'd been eating for the last four years.

He grabbed his duffel bag from his car and walked towards the house. He circled around the back and climbed the stairs to his old apartment above the garage. It was just past midnight and his flight had been delayed due to a thunderstorm in Colorado. He was exhausted.

Dropping his bag inside his door, he took a few steps

into the apartment and knew instantly that he wasn't alone. Every muscle in his body tensed as he scanned the dark room. In the last few years he'd been in plenty of fights and as he prepared his body for the blows, his mind refused to acknowledge the signal of the sweet scents that his nose was sending him.

The first blow skimmed his jaw, sending him back a few steps. When he reached out with his fist, he thought he would connect with something, but he hit only air. The blow to his gut took him by surprise, and he reached out and grabbed what he could of his attacker.

When he grabbed ahold of clothes, he stepped back to flip his assailant over, but tripped on his duffel bag and ended up on the ground. He'd taken his assaulter down with him, so he rolled a few times until he ended up on top.

"What are you doing in my house?" he demanded at the same time a fist came up and connected with his left eye. He moaned with pain just as the body underneath him stilled.

"Your house?"

It was a woman's voice, causing him to momentarily drop his guard.

She shoved his shoulder and leg hard until he fell off her. He landed on the floor, holding his throbbing left eye.

Then the lights flipped on and thereby the door to his apartment stood a warrior goddess. Her long red hair flowed down past her breasts, which were covered nicely with a teal tank top and matching shorts.

"Travis?" She stood looking down at him.

He dropped his hand away from his face and looked at her with watery eyes. "Do I know you?"

She nodded her head and put her hands on her hips. "Holly Bridles." He just looked at her. "I run the bookstore."

"Sure, you do," he said getting up off the ground slowly. "That doesn't explain what you're doing in my house."

She sighed. "I live here." She looked around the apartment and for the first time, he realized it was clean. Clean, clean. Everything of his was gone except the furniture his parents had bought him when he'd moved out of the main house.

He groaned. "That's just great." He turned and looked at her again.

She was still standing by the front door, and he wondered why his father would have rented the place out to a librarian.

"I guess I didn't know he'd rented the place out."

"He didn't," she said quickly. His eyebrows shot up in question. "I'm not renting the place."

Well, that cleared it up, he thought. It had been bound to happen. After all, the ink on his parents' divorce had been dry for almost three years now. He looked at the woman's skimpy outfit and smiled a little. Way to go, dad, he thought. Then he frowned as she stepped further into the light. What was a man in his late sixties doing with someone so young?

"I didn't know you were going to be back." She crossed her arms over her chest, no doubt because he'd been staring at those lovely tits of hers.

He blinked and stepped closer. Her hands dropped and rested by her sides in fists, reminding him that his eye was throbbing. He wondered how such a small package of a woman could pack such a big punch with those tiny fists.

"I guess I'll head over to the main house until we sort this all out." He bent to pick up his duffel bag. When he stood back up, he noticed her biting her bottom lip with worry. He turned and walked out of his apartment without another word.

Okay, he told himself on the short walk towards the back door of the big house, I need a new to-do list. As he opened the back door of the massive house, he listed things off in his mind. Get rid of dad's hussy, which was really too bad since he could have used the distraction while he was in town; sell the house; and get the hell out of Fairplay, Texas.

Holly stood in her doorway and bit her bottom lip. Travis was back. What did that mean? Was he going to kick her out of the apartment? Without the store being open, she doubted she could afford to rent another place. At least until the doors opened again, she needed to stay put.

The reading of Mr. Nolan's will had been postponed until Travis made it back into town. Until then, it had been agreed that the construction on the store would continue. Shutting the door, she leaned up against the cool wood and rested her head back, closing her eyes. She was in deep trouble. What if there wasn't anything about their agreement in Mr. Nolan's will? Would Travis hold up his father's wishes? Would she be kicked to the curb? What about her store? Would construction stop?

Shaking her head clear of the million questions running

through it, she walked back towards the bedroom and grabbed the water bottle she'd gotten up to get. Thankfully, it had caused her to hear the front door open. She knew the door had been locked and bolted—something she did every night—which meant he had a key to the place. She walked towards the door, locked it again, and snapped the chain on for good measure.

Travis was trouble. Had been most of his life and probably would be until the day he died. Too bad, she thought, crawling into bed. The man had a body like the gods and a face to melt even the hardest hearts. She sighed and closed her eyes, burying her face into the pillow. What she wouldn't give to feel a good man on top of her like he'd been a short while ago. Giggling to herself, she decided she had gone too long without a date.

Then she frowned when she remembered she lived in a small town and there were no good men to date. Closing her eyes tighter, she tried to get the feeling of being that close to a man out of her mind.

She woke early the next morning and headed in to check on how construction was going. Since Mr. Nolan's death, she spent most of her time making sure everything was staying on track—helping with ordering and organizing the materials, coordinating the construction crews, solving any issues or questions they had during the entire process. Some of the men had even given her her own hard hat and tool belt.

She knew that leaving early would make it harder for Travis to track her down and try to kick her to the curb. Since she was working on only a few hours of sleep, she was having a hard time concentrating. She stood off to the side and watched the men work and tried to imagine what the place would look like once it was finished.

The day didn't get any better when, an hour past lunch, a water pipe broke in the apartment and started leaking downstairs. It took every man on site to finally clear the standing water on the cement floor so the workers could continue hanging the drywall. Thankfully, the damage had been contained to just a small spot that was already being patched.

She stood in what would be her new storeroom, looking up at the work the drywaller had done when she felt a tap on her shoulder. She turned expecting to see a workman but was shocked to see Travis standing there looking down at her with a frown and a very black and swollen left eye.

"What's all this?" he demanded with a frown.

Her eyebrows shot up in question. He had his hands on his hips and a very impatient look on his face. He was wearing a dress shirt and dress pants. Even his shoes were shiny and new looking. His dark hair had been combed back and he'd shaved since she'd seen him last night. "You shouldn't be in here without a hard hat." She walked over to the back doorway and grabbed a yellow hat and handed it over to him.

He set it on his head and demanded in a louder voice, which rose above all the pounding and sawing, "What is this?" He motioned around him.

"This is my store." She frowned. "Remember?"

"Your bookstore?"

She nodded. "Yes."

He took a deep breath and rubbed his forehead. "What I mean is, why is it under construction?"

She frowned. "Because the wiring in the building was older than the hills, and there was still roofing damage from the tornado, and…"

"I mean," he ground out, interrupting her, "why is my father paying for all of this?" He yelled over the loud noises coming from a few feet away. She was used to the noises by now after being on site every day for the last month.

"Because it's his building," she yelled back, looking at him like he was crazy.

He grabbed her arm and marched her out of the back door. Here there was even more noise since other men were using table saws and nail guns. He stopped and looked around, then continued to walk her towards the little garden area she had along the side of the building. She'd been raising tomatoes and squash and had a little picnic table and swing along a tall fence.

"Why is my father paying a lot of money to have you rebuild your store?" he finally said, dropping her arm and waving what she assumed were the bills.

"Because it's his building and he had a vision." She crossed her arms over her chest.

"Great," he said, rolling his eyes. "Now he was having visions."

She frowned. "Your father wanted to rebuild the bookstore."

"I'm sure he did." He looked her over. She had put on her standard construction clothes—old jeans, button-up blouse, and an old pair of boots. She'd tied her hair in two long braids, which lay across her shoulders out of her way.

"What does that mean?" she asked, putting her hands on her hips.

He laughed. "Listen, you're very attractive and I'm sure you had your usefulness when my father was alive, but there's just no way I'm going to continue all this." He motioned towards the building.

She was shocked. He was going to take it all away from her.

"I don't know what kind of…arrangement you and my father had, but he's gone now and you can expect that anything he was giving you won't be coming from me." He turned to go.

"I'm sorry?" she said to his back.

He turned and looked at her, then sighed and turned back. "If I was sticking around town, maybe I'd help you out, but I'm not. I'm heading over to the lawyer's office right now and putting all this"—he motioned to the building— "on the market. So if I were you, I'd pack up what you can and get going, because if you're still on my property by tonight, I'll call the cops."

She lost the last thread of her temper at that moment. "How dare you." She took a step closer to him. "Your father was a great man, a man with a vision for this town, and in one day you plan to wipe out everything he's worked hard for?"

He took a step closer to her. "You'll want to be careful what you say to me." His eyes bore into hers.

She took another step closer to him until they were almost nose-to-nose. Well, they would have been if he wasn't a foot taller than her. She blinked back her anger before finally speaking.

"You're heading over to Grant's now?" she asked, throwing him off balance.

Grant normally worked out of his house, but since they

had a daughter, he was in the office more and more. He claimed it was hard to take a business call when there was a kid screaming in the background, but everyone knew that Alex, his wife, had kicked him out so he would actually get some work done instead of playing with their daughter all the time.

When he finally nodded, she said, "Good, I'll just walk over there with you." She turned and started walking down the street.

He laughed and followed her. "Why? Do you really think that my father left you anything?"

"No, I know he didn't." She glanced over her shoulder at him.

"Then why tag along?" He kept in step with her easily, noticing that she marched a little faster when he was beside her.

"Because I know what he wanted, and I can only hope that he had the brains to put it all down on paper before he left us," she said, a little breathless.

By the time they walked into Grant Holton's office a few blocks away, she was completely out of breath. Her face was red from the heat and some of her hair had come loose from the braids.

When she marched back towards the office, Travis followed. Knocking on the door, she stepped in without waiting for an answer. Grant was on the phone and when he saw her, he nodded and smiled. When he saw Travis, he quickly apologized and hung up the phone.

"Travis?" He stood and held out his hand. "It's good to have you back in town."

Travis was completely floored. This was the man whom his mother had shot and tried to kill. He'd heard that Grant had married Alexis shortly after Travis had left Fairplay. Now the man was actually being nice, like none of it had ever happened.

"Grant." He shook his hand and stood there like he didn't know what to say next.

There were pictures of Alex, Grant, and their children all over the office. Travis glanced at a few, but then turned his eyes towards the floor. It was too hard to see Alex in those pictures, happily holding a chubby baby.

"Travis and I would like to know what's in his father's will," Holly said, crossing her arms over her chest.

"Now, Holly, we've been through this a dozen times. I can't tell you what's in Mr. Nolan's will unless Travis here"—he nodded towards him— "says it's okay."

She glared at him until finally, he nodded. "I'll allow it, I suppose." What harm could it cause? After all, there was no way his father had left anything to this woman.

"Fine. If you'll take a seat, I'll just pull it up." Grant sat back behind his desk. "Did you just get into town?" he asked him.

Travis shook his head. "Last night," he said, looking down at his fingernails, not wanting to make eye contact with the man.

"I hope your trip was good. We're really sorry about your dad; he was a good man."

Travis glanced up at Grant quickly. "Thanks," he said and then looked back down at his fingers.

"Here it is," Grant said, getting both of their attention.

He skimmed over the computer screen then turned to them. "I'll cut to the chase." He looked up at him. "What it says in here is that the house and all the assets go to you, Travis…"

Travis smiled and glanced over at Holly.

"…After completion of any current projects." Grant leaned back in his chair. "There are explicit orders that you oversee them until completion or you forfeit everything."

"What?" he said, sitting forward. "What does that mean? What projects?"

"Well, your father started a few of them over the last few months. As I can see, you already know about the bookstore. He also started renovation work on the old theater, and on building a new park area just outside of town." He glanced at the screen again.

"I don't understand." Travis stood up.

"Earlier this year, your father talked to me about wanting to put some of his money back into the town. He started a few smaller projects at first, like a fresh coat of paint on town hall, getting a few new park benches around town, and some new streetlights. Then Holly approached him about updating the bookstore and her apartment. I guess that started him thinking about some of the other projects he'd been putting off."

"Can't they just continue without me?"

Grant shook his head. "Your father made it clear that if you didn't oversee the projects personally, they would stop completely."

"Good, then stop them, I don't care." He turned to go.

"If they stop, you'll be left with nothing. Everything your father owned will go to the town, so we can finish the projects without you," Grant said.

Travis stopped, his hand on the doorknob. He needed his inheritance if he was going to get out of the world he'd been in the last few years. He was getting tired and wanted to do something more with his life. He spun around and glared at the woman he thought was the cause of his father's crazy scheme. "This was all your doing."

Holly stood up and glared right back at him. "Don't be silly."

"Travis, Holly had nothing to do with this. There's a note here." He held out a sealed envelope. "From your father."

"You mean I'm stuck in this town until all of his little projects are done?"

Grant nodded and handed him the note. "If you want your inheritance, you are. There is one more thing in here." Grant looked down at Holly. "Holly stays in the apartment, rent-free until the building is done. Once the building is completed, there are more instructions that I'm not at liberty to discuss until such time."

Travis walked out of the building without another word. He stood on the sidewalk and ripped open his father's note.

Son,

I know how hard the last few years have been on you. I wanted you to know that I'm proud of you. I've checked up on you and know that you've cleaned up your life. I couldn't be prouder of you.

I'm asking you for a favor now. If you're reading this, it means that I have left some unfinished business in town. These people deserve our thanks. They have been there for us in our time of need. You may not have seen it, but each and every person in this town is behind you.

I'll ask this last thing from you. Please finish what I have started so the town and the wonderful people in it can heal.

I love you, son.

He was trapped. No matter what he did, he had a sinking feeling that there was no way he would ever leave Fairplay again.

CHAPTER 2

Holly walked up the stairs to the place she'd been calling home for the last few months and sighed when she saw Travis standing at the top. She didn't want another fight right now. It had been a long day filled with troubling issues and she was very tired.

After their trip to Grant's, she'd come back to find that the water leak had been a more major issue than they had thought. Now they were ripping out most of the drywall in the back storage room so all the plumbing could be checked and fixed. It was going to set them back a few days, if not more.

"What do you want?" she said, not even looking at him as she hoisted her groceries to her other hand, so she could unlock the door.

"I need to get a few things out of my apartment," he said, grabbing one of her bags before she dropped it.

"There's nothing of yours left in here." She unlocked the door and walked in.

"Where's all my stuff then?" He followed her, looking around the clean space.

"The garage. Your father had it all moved down there." She set the bags on the countertop. When he set the other bags next to hers, she stepped back.

He started to walk out, but she saw something in his eyes and stopped him.

"Travis?" He stopped at the doorway and looked back at her. "I'm really sorry about your father." When he nodded, she continued. "His last thoughts were of you."

He turned and took a step towards her. "You were with him?"

She nodded. "We were in the bookstore, checking out the construction."

He frowned and looked down at his feet. It was the first emotion she'd ever seen on him other than anger.

"He had such wonderful plans for you, for the town." She took another step towards him. "He'd talked a lot in his last few weeks about you coming home."

He turned to go without another word.

"We weren't lovers." She knew he'd been thinking it since the first night. "Your parents were my godparents." She waited for his response, but he just continued to walk out. "You're going to have to talk to me sometime," she called after him.

He stopped on the stairs and looked up at her. "I'll stay to finish my father's projects, and then I'm putting every-thing on the market and getting the hell out of this damn town." He turned and continued walking down the stairs.

She didn't know what forced her to follow. Maybe it was the lost look in his eyes when she'd talked about his dad. He'd disappeared into the dark garage through the side door and when she pulled open the door, the darkness was almost blinding. She stumbled a little and almost fell down the small step just inside the door. Strong arms grabbed her by the waist and held her steady.

"Thanks," she mumbled, just before he pushed her back against the closed door of the garage.

"Why are you here?" It sounded like a growl.

Her heart skipped a beat. She'd always thought of him like a bear, even more so since he'd returned home. Now he was a caged one. She wondered why she'd willingly walked into a dark place, knowing he was in there.

"You know why." She threw her chin up, daring him to challenge her again. She'd held her own last night, and he had the shiner to prove it.

He looked down at her in the darkness. She could see his dark eyes boring into her and something in her told her not to blink or look away.

Finally, he dropped his arms from her shoulders and stepped back. "Leave me alone." He turned and flipped on the overhead lights, which popped on with a loud hum.

When he began looking through the pile of boxes against the back wall, she walked over and watched. "If you tell me what you're looking for, maybe I can help."

He turned and glared at her. "Go away." He threw a box in the pile he'd already gone through.

She put her hands on her hips and frowned. Fine, if he didn't want to be neighborly, that was okay with her. She turned to go, but then stopped to peek under the sheet that was covering an old car. Seeing what was underneath, she gasped and yanked at the cover.

"Leave that alone," he barked and reached for the cover.

"It's beautiful," she said, tossing the car cover aside. "Why is it sitting in the garage, collecting dust?" She walked up and down the cherry red 1967 Mustang convertible. There were thick black stripes running down the front hood. As she walked around it, she trailed her finger along the glossy paint job. The interior was black leather and looked like it had recently been redone. The wheels were chrome and looked new. She bent and looked at a small dent in the fender and made a disapproving sound. "Too bad." She shook her head.

"Where did that dent come from?" he said right behind her, causing her to jump a little. She looked over her shoulder.

"Is this yours?" She nodded towards the car.

"No." He frowned.

"Your father's?" she asked. When he shook his head no, she asked, "Your mother's, then?" When he nodded this time, she understood. "Did your dad fix it up for her?"

He nodded. "We spent almost six years rebuilding it for her. It was a surprise for their twenty-fifth anniversary." He walked around the car and sighed. "So many hours locked up in the garage downtown that he'd rented. Just the two of us." She watched him walk around the car as he talked about his time with his father, his eyes sad and downcast. "When we finally pulled it into the driveway"— he closed his eyes— "it was the most exciting thing in the world."

"Did your mother love it?" She smiled, looking at the car. "I know I would have."

When he didn't say anything, she turned and looked at him. He was staring at her with a frown on his face. Without saying a word, he grabbed up the cover and tossed it over the car. "Don't you have somewhere else to be?"

She crossed her arms over her chest and glared at him. "Are you always this sour?" He continued to frown at her until she threw up her hands in frustration and turned to go.

"You throw a pretty good punch for a girl," he said at her back, causing her to spin around and nod at him. "Where'd you learn to do that?" he asked, leaning back against the covered car, crossing his arms over his chest like she'd just done. On him, the effect was quite different. His muscles stretched his white T-shirt taut, showing the ripples on his arms and chest rather nicely. She blinked a few times and tried to focus on his face, but when she looked at him, he had a smile on his lips, telling her that he knew exactly what the sight of him was doing to her.

"My father," she finally got out.

His eyebrows shot up. "I thought your old man died a long time ago."

She nodded. "When I was ten. But before he…" She looked down at her hands. "Before he died, he taught me how to fight. How to protect myself."

"So it's true? About him?"

She looked back into his dark brown eyes and saw something there she hadn't before. He looked tired. Tired and curious.

"What?"

"That your old man was Samson," he said, leaning closer to her. "The stuff boxing legends were made of."

She laughed. "That's old news. Haven't you read my book?"

"Your book?" He tilted his head with a frown.

She nodded. "It came out earlier this year. *Serving Life*. It's all about my father. His experience in the Navy and how he became Samson, the unbeatable boxer." She smiled. "It goes on to tell about his struggles and why he chose to come back home to Fairplay and settle down, marrying my mother and having me."

He leaned up. "You seriously wrote a book?" She nodded. "I guess I'll have to check it out then."

She looked at him as he stood in the dark garage. "If you tell me what it is you're looking for; I can help find it."

He glanced over at the large pile of boxes. "My guitar."

She laughed harder than she had in days.

"What?" He smiled and took a step closer to her.

"You were looking for a guitar in a box?" She held her sides and smiled at him. His smile dropped a little.

"I guess I wasn't really thinking." He started to frown and glanced at the box.

"What about that?" She pointed to the guitar case sitting above their head on a shelf.

He smiled and then chuckled. "You throw me off, I guess." He pulled a box over, stood up on it, and grabbed the guitar from the shelf.

"I didn't know you played."

"I used to do a lot of things." He shrugged his shoulders and set the case on the covered hood of the car and opened it. He pulled the guitar out and looked at it. It was an older model, but the wood still shined like new.

"It's beautiful."

He nodded and looked at her. "It was my grandfather's."

"Oh? Are you going to play again?"

He shook his head. "No, I'm going to sell it." He set the guitar back in the case and shut it.

"Oh." She frowned. How many times in the past had she thought about selling her father's items? Times when she didn't know if she would be able to pay rent, or times when she had a large unexpected bill. But she had stuck to her guns and held onto all of his things and eventually, everything had worked out.

"If you're hurting for money, I can…"

He turned on her and the look on his face said it all. Butt out. She stopped talking and took a step back.

"Sorry, I was just trying—"

"I know what you were doing. I don't need your help." He grabbed the case and walked out without another word.

He walked back into the house, and Holly couldn't help but wonder what he was going through.

Travis set down the guitar case on the countertop and looked around the large kitchen. What was he going to do? He was stuck here with no access to his money until his father's projects were done. Why was the old man punishing him? They had always gotten along great. He supposed it was because he had taken off after his mom was arrested.

He sat on a bar stool and looked off towards the stove. He could still picture his mother there, making her fried chicken or baking a pie. He closed his eyes. Why had she betrayed them?

Insanity. Did it run in the family? That was a question

he'd been asking himself for the last four years. He'd done everything he could to prove to himself that he wasn't crazy, but in the end, he thought that everything he'd done had taken him one step closer to it.

Then an image of Holly came to his mind. She hadn't looked at him like he was crazy for wanting to sell his grandfather's guitar. What he'd seen in her eyes was sadness and understanding. He didn't know why, but he was finding it harder and harder to be around her. Maybe it was because he knew that she'd had a special bond with his father before he'd died. Or maybe it was because she was a tight little sexy package that annoyed him every time she opened her mouth. He'd even thought about kissing her to shut her up, but thankfully he'd come to his senses before that had happened.

He'd learned to put aside his desires in the last few years. He looked down at his fists and frowned. How many times had he used his hands to try and focus his body and mind? To convince himself that he was something more than a crazy woman's son? He'd finally learned to discipline his body and his mind. So much so that he'd almost forgotten what it was like to be with a woman or to take something he wanted.

Just then his cell phone rang. When he looked down at the number, he sighed. He had known his agent wouldn't wait too long. Not even his father's death could suspend his obligations.

"Hey, Randy." He rubbed his forehead and thought about the headache that was growing.

"Travis, my man. Where are you at?" Randy always had a way of getting to the point.

"I'm still at home. I have a few loose ends I have to tie up."

"Oh, man, that doesn't really work for me. I need you back in Vegas next week. Tuesday night we have a rematch with Steve Cann. Listen, I have it all set up. You've got a room at—"

"Sorry, Randy, I won't be able to make it." He closed his eyes, knowing what was coming next.

"Man, I understand. It's just a shame, you know, after all, I've done for you. Well, if you'll just send me the money you owe me, then we can part ways." Travis knew the old drill. There was no way Randy would ever let him go. Not really.

"I don't have it yet. My old man has me jumping through a few hoops before I can get to the cash. I can pay you off in a few months."

"Travis, you have until Monday to either show up in Vegas or wire me the money." Randy hung up and Travis knew he was screwed.

He felt like throwing his phone. He looked across the room at his grandfather's guitar. Pawning it would only get him a few hundred dollars and a broken heart, knowing something so valuable to him was gone. What he needed was a few thousand dollars, and he had no idea how to get it all by Monday. He knew one thing—leaving town wasn't going to be a possibility, not this soon.

He felt like punching something. After all, it's what he'd been doing for therapy for the last four years. He usually felt more leveled after hitting something with his fists. Heading back out to the garage, he pulled out his old punching bag and hung it on the hook on the back porch. Pulling his gloves from his bag, he stripped down to his shorts and started wailing on the bag, trying to come up with a plan.

An hour later, his fists stung, his muscles screamed, and he felt like he could finally focus on coming up with a plan to pay off his agent and get out of the world of underground cage fighting.

CHAPTER 3

"What do you mean he's taken over?" Holly stood in the front of her store. The workers looked like they didn't know what to do next. She'd shown up that morning and found them all standing around. She had hunted down the foreman, Roger, who had quickly informed her that Travis was now in charge of the site, and he'd stopped all work until he could inspect everything that had been done so far.

Roger shrugged his shoulders. "He was here before I got here this morning, looking around."

"Where is he now?" she asked.

"I think he's upstairs." He nodded his head towards the stairs.

She marched away without another word. Her anger carried her up the stairs and through the door to her apartment. Travis was standing in the middle of her living room, a clipboard in his hands, and a frown on his face.

"What do you think you're doing?" She stopped in front of him, her hands on her hips as she glared at him.

He glanced up, then back down at his notepad. "I'm doing what my father asked of me. I'm taking over the project."

"The hell you are." She reached for the clipboard. "This is my project. I don't need you here. Why don't you go work on the theater or the park?" She turned to go.

"I'm not going anywhere. I'll deal with those projects as well. But for now"—he walked over and took his clipboard from her— "I'm dealing with this project. And, from the looks of it, you need my help."

She glared at him. "What do you mean?"

He chuckled. "There are too many issues to discuss standing here. Why don't we meet at Mama's diner in"—he glanced down at his watch— "an hour. I have to tell the men the changes that need to be made." He turned to walk into her bedroom, but she stopped him.

"What changes?" She followed him. "You are *not* making changes without telling me first."

He turned and glanced at her over his shoulder, then shrugged. "Fine." He handed her the clipboard. "These are just a few that I've noted so far. I'll want a more thorough walkthrough later today when there aren't workers standing around wasting my money."

She looked down at the clipboard and started reading. She had to admit that he had a few valid ideas. Some she hadn't thought of, others she didn't like, but still, they were good ideas.

"I don't need a sink in the storeroom." She moved to mark it off the list.

"You have a fridge in the room. I'm assuming you're going to use it as a break room."

She looked up at him and nodded. "So?"

He chuckled. "What if you have an employee who wants a cup of tea? Where would they get the water?"

She frowned. "The bathroom is a few feet away."

He made a tsking noise and shook his head. "A proper break room needs a sink and a microwave alongside the fridge."

She frowned, looking down at the list. Okay, so he had a point. "Well, I don't want two bathrooms' downstairs. I only need one."

"You only needed one when you had a bookstore. From what I've heard, this is going to be a coffeehouse and wine bar now, as well as a bookstore." When she nodded her head, he continued. "You'll have more customers in here at one time and state law requires that you have both male and female restrooms for every one hundred and -fifty people. Once it's done, downstairs will be zoned for up to two hundred occupancies. You need two restrooms." He took the list from her.

She looked at him and frowned. "How do you know that?"

He glanced up at her. "My father was an architect. He made me take some online classes right out of high school." He turned and walked into what was going to be her new master bathroom. "This was a waste of space."

She followed him. "My bathroom?" She looked around the large room and imagined how it would look a few months from now. There was going to be a large garden tub, a huge glass-walled shower with stone tiles, and a double sink with marble countertops along the inside wall. The large frosted window would let in natural light and give the whole room an updated look.

"You don't need near this amount of space. A simple

shower/tub combo would have been better." He started writing it down.

"Don't you dare change a thing in here." She reached for his clipboard, only to have him pull it away. "We're keeping this room the way I want it."

He held the clipboard away from her. "I say we change it to a tub combo."

She reached for the clipboard again, but he held it out of her range.

"We don't need you around here. Everything is going just fine without you. Everything stays the way it is." She glared at him and held her hand out for his clipboard.

His eyebrows shot up, and then a slow smile crossed his lips. She tried not to focus on the fact that he had sexy lips. She hadn't realized they were so close to one another, not until she felt his breath on her face and realized she could see the dark speckles in his eyes. She held perfectly still and held her breath, not wanting to move or make a sound.

Before she could respond, he'd dropped the clipboard, put his hands on her shoulders, and pulled her closer. Then his lips were on hers and she lost all of the fight she'd had moments before. When his hands tightened on her shoulders and his mouth softened over hers, a moan escaped her closed lips, allowing his tongue to dart inside her mouth for a taste. He tasted like sugar, and his lips were warm and soft against hers; she couldn't stop herself from holding him closer. His shoulders were strong, and she enjoyed the play of muscles down his arms as her nails dug into his shirtsleeve.

He pulled away for a moment, his dark eyes scanning her face as he stilled a breath from her lips.

"You set me off." He shook his head. "God help me." His mouth descended again, but just then they heard the door to her apartment open and they jumped apart quickly.

By the time Roger walked into the room, Travis had his clipboard in his hands and was frowning down at his list. Holly still hadn't fully recovered, so she was looking out the window, trying to look like she hadn't just been kissed until her toes had curled.

"Is everything okay in here, boss?" Roger stopped just inside the doorway.

"Yeah, gather the men. I have a few changes." Travis looked at her. "I'll see you at Mama's in an hour." He dismissed her without another word. She stood in her bathroom and watched the two men leave her apartment and wondered what she was going to do now.

She looked around the rooms for a moment until she felt her body stop shaking. Then she walked down the street to the clinic in hopes that Melissa, her best friend, was at work so she could get another woman's perspective on what had just happened.

What the hell had he done? Why had he let his guard down around her? He tried to concentrate as he told Roger and the men about the changes he wanted. For some reason, he just couldn't bring himself to make the changes that he knew were needed in Holly's bathroom, even though the current plans would waste a few thousand dollars.

Forty minutes later, as he walked out of the construction zone and headed down the street towards the diner, he tried to build up his defenses again. He did the breathing exercises he'd learned. He focused his mind and tried to clear all bad thoughts from it.

Man, he wished he had a cigarette. He stopped on the sidewalk and blinked a few times. That was the first time in almost three years that he'd thought about smoking. This town was a bad influence on him. He needed to finish his job and get the hell out of it quickly.

When he walked into Mama's, he tried to hide the groan that almost escaped him. In the back-corner booth were two of his close high school friends, Billy Jackson and Corey Park. They were the two guys he'd gotten in the most trouble with in his life, and he'd been avoiding the men since his return. There were so many stories of the three of them causing problems that he didn't know where to start. He had hoped to be in and out of town before either of them knew he was back.

But as he stood in the doorway and the door chime faded, both men looked over, and he saw acknowledgment cross their faces. When Billy stood and waved him over, he knew he wouldn't be able to avoid talking to them. He glanced over and saw Holly sitting at a table across the room on the other side. He walked towards the back booth and nodded to where Holly sat, waiting for him.

"Hey," he said as he shook hands with Billy and Corey.

"Man, we didn't know you were back," Corey said, patting him hard on the back. "We're sorry about your old man. He was really cool to us."

"Yeah, he always helped bail us out," Billy piped in. "Why don't you sit? We were just having some lunch then we were going to head to Corey's old man's cabin and party."

It was the same story. Corey's father owned a hunting

cabin along the lake. He couldn't count the times the three of them had partied there with girls, booze, and occasionally drugs. From the sounds of it, Corey and Billy hadn't changed at all in the last four years since he'd left town.

"I can't, I've got a meeting." He looked over to where Holly sat, watching them. Her blue eyes searched his from across the room. He knew he'd thrown her off balance earlier. Hell, she'd thrown him off balance by kissing him back. It would have been better if she'd pulled away and thrown another one of her power punches in his direction. He would have felt safer than he did now.

"With the book nerd?" Corey chuckled. "Man, you have changed."

He looked at his friends. "Some of us are trying to better ourselves." His friends laughed.

"Well, the invitation is always open," Billy said, sitting back down as the waitress delivered their food. "Stop by sometime. We're sure glad to see you back in town."

He nodded, then turned and walked over to where Holly sat, a plate of French fries in front of her, untouched.

"Sorry, I'm late." He sat down, putting the clipboard on the table next to him.

"It's okay." She looked off towards his friends. "Are you going to hang with those two again?" she asked, frowning.

He looked towards his old friends, who were now making a scene by squirting ketchup at one another. "Hadn't planned on it." He frowned and turned back towards her as the waitress came to take his order. He ordered the potato soup and a salad. He knew he had to cut back on calories since he wasn't training right now. His stomach growled and demanded that he order more, but he'd learned to discipline himself.

"What other changes have you made?" She reached for his clipboard and he let her take it. He sipped his water as she read over the new list.

He'd crossed a few items off and had added a few others during his meeting with Roger. He felt the building was in good hands after talking to the contractor. At least his father had done his research and hired the best around.

She frowned as she read over his list. He liked the little crease that appeared between her eyebrows. She had a cute little dimple near the corner of her mouth that he wanted to taste again. If he focused, he could still taste her sweet lips on his, feel her soft body next to his. He closed his eyes and tried to focus on something else.

"I guess I can live with these changes." She interrupted his thoughts. He looked over at her. He'd been expecting a fight from her.

"Really?" He sat back as his food was delivered.

"Sure. I mean, some of these Roger had suggested." She pointed to a few items on his list. "Here, he wanted the bookshelves to go along this back wall instead of this one. We'd talked about redoing the fireplace and converting it to gas, so that was already in the works." She glanced up at him. "I thought about adding a small stage, here." She pulled out a floor plan from her bag and pointed to it. He scooted closer and looked down at the paper, trying to see where she meant.

"In the back corner?"

She nodded and looked at him.

"Why did you kiss me?" The question threw him off balance. He continued to look at her, not knowing how to answer it. "I mean; I know why I kissed you back. It's been almost a year since I've gone on a date. But why did you kiss me?" she asked again.

He was mesmerized by her eyes, and he couldn't stop himself from watching her bite her bottom lip with worry. "I wanted to." He shrugged his shoulders. She sighed and leaned back when he made no move to explain himself further. "A stage for what?" he asked, causing her to blink a few times and refocus on the meeting.

"Bands, poetry readings, book signings." She shrugged and reached for a French fry. "There are lots of reasons to have a small stage."

"I guess we could make it work. I'll talk to Roger after lunch."

"I can do it." She took another fry and nibbled on it. The slow motion was hypnotizing him.

"No, I'll do it. I'm in charge now." He leaned in and started eating his soup and salad, wishing desperately for a cheeseburger instead.

"Is there something wrong with the soup?" she asked. He realized he'd been frowning down at his bowl.

"No, just wishing it was a cheeseburger instead."

She smiled. "I know what you mean. I had a New Year's resolution that I've been good at keeping so far. I've only eaten fish this year, no other meat." She shook her head. "I'm dying for a burger or a chicken breast. But I've lost ten pounds so far and kept it off."

"I try to save meat for when I'm not training."

Her eyebrows shot up. "Boxing?" When he just looked at her, she blushed a little. He liked the look of her cheeks turning pink. "I saw you hitting the bag yesterday."

He smiled a little. "Yeah, I've been fighting the last

few years. It helps me stay focused." He frowned, remembering his conversation with Randy.

"Really?" She leaned forward a little. "Where?"

He shook his head, wanting the conversation to end. "I'll talk to Roger about adding the stage." He tossed a few dollars on the table and stood up.

"Don't bother. I'm heading over there now." She looked at him.

"No, you're not. A construction zone is no place for a woman."

She laughed at him. He looked down at her like she was crazy.

"Listen." She stood and crossed her arms over her chest, and he realized how much smaller she was then he'd thought. The top of her head reached just below his shoulders. She was already thin and the fact that she'd just confessed to losing ten pounds this past year had him frowning. She didn't need to lose weight; if anything, she could stand to gain a few pounds. He liked his women soft. "I've been on site since the first sledgehammer was swung. I have no intention of leaving it until it's finished. This is my store, my apartment. If you want me to leave, you'll just have to get used to disappointment."

He didn't feel like arguing in front of everyone in the diner, so he grabbed her arm and started walking out.

"Wait." She pulled on his arm, stopping him. "You can't push me around." She stopped and grabbed her bag from the floor near her chair, and then reached over and grabbed another fry from her almost-empty plate. Then she turned and followed him. "Now I'm ready." She marched to the door and opened it and then turned and waited for him to join her. He tried not to chuckle.

As they walked back towards the store, she talked about some of the other changes she'd been thinking of.

"I had a list going of new items, but after your father died, I didn't think I should change anymore." She bit her lip and he again found himself watching the sweet motion. "But now that you're here"—she looked over at him with a slight smile— "I would like to go over a few of them with you."

"As long as it doesn't slow down the process." And didn't cost him too much more. In the back of his mind, he was thinking of the bottom line—what would it cost him and what could he gain from it once he put the place up on the market. He wasn't telling Holly, but after construction on her place and the theater were done, he was going to slap a "for sale" sign on them both as fast as he could.

"No, they shouldn't. Most are just small items."

"Like a stage?" He looked at her in question.

"Well, okay, that one was big." She smiled up at him and he found himself smiling back.

Just then they heard a car horn honk, and Savannah Douglas pulled her white Jeep to their side of the road.

olly held her breath as Savannah got out of the Jeep and walked towards them. The last time she'd talked to the woman, she'd been drunk and had given Savannah a broken nose. Ever since that night a few months ago, she'd been avoiding the woman. Savannah for her part had stayed in hiding. Her father had tried to sue the Rusty Rail, the only bar in Fairplay, claiming that Savannah had tripped on a broken tile instead of being almost knocked out by a woman half her size.

"You're back in town," she exclaimed right before she threw herself at Travis and kissed him square on the lips.

Holly felt her stomach turn and tried to look away, but for some reason, her eyes were glued to the couple.

Travis with his classic rugged cowboy look, his dark hair, dark eyes, and the sexy cleft in his chin. Savannah with her long, blonde, perfectly styled hair, and her large breasts, which were always highlighted in tight, expensive clothes. In the last few months, since the nose incident,

Holly had noticed that she'd gained some weight, but she was still gorgeous.

"Yeah, just got back the other day," he said, taking a step away from Savannah and looking over at Holly. She'd taken a few steps away and was trying to escape the awkwardness that she felt.

"You remember Holly." He motioned towards her, and she wanted to be anywhere but on Main Street with Savannah Douglas and Travis Nolan, easily the two people in Fairplay that the town had talked about the most. Travis and Savannah's affair had caused a lot of loss in the small town; his mother had lost her sanity, his father had lost his job, and two of her best friends has almost lost their lives.

Savannah didn't even spare her a glance. Instead, she pulled Travis closer and ran her hands over his shoulders. "It's so good that you're back in town to stay. You simply must come to the house for dinner," she purred, leaving Holly wishing she could make her voice sound that sexy. Maybe with some practice?

"I'm not staying," he said, pulling her arms from his shoulders. "I'm sorry, Savannah, but I have some business to tend to right now."

Savannah's lips formed into a pout and Holly noticed that the emotion didn't reach her eyes. "Well, okay. How about I stop by later?"

Travis shook his head. "No, not this time. I'll see you around." He turned and looked at her. "Ready?"

She didn't know what to say, so she just nodded and matched his steps as they walked to the bookstore together. She desperately wanted to turn around and stick her tongue out at Savannah, but she knew better than to stoop to that woman's level. Besides, she was no longer a child and didn't want Travis to see her acting like one. But part of her had to admit, it felt good to see Savannah struggle.

"I heard you two got into a fight recently." He looked down at her. "Broke her nose?"

She swallowed and nodded. Everyone in town knew about the fight, which was one of the reasons Mr. Douglas's attempt to sue the Rusty Rail had failed. "She talked bad about someone I love."

He chuckled. "Savannah is always talking bad about someone." He glanced at her sideways. "I hope he appreciated what you did."

She stopped and looked at him. "He?"

He stopped and turned to her, then nodded.

She laughed. "The 'he' is a 'she.' Melissa Holton."

His eyes shot up, and she watched as understanding flooded them. "Ohhhh," he said, and she couldn't help but laugh.

"My best friend, not my lover." She giggled.

"Oh," he repeated, and he smiled. "Well, you never know. I've been to a few places where you always had to question it."

"Oh?" she said as they began to walk again. "Like where?"

He shrugged his shoulders. "Mainly Vegas. I spent my first year after leaving here there."

"I've always wanted to go. I've heard it's fun." She sighed and stood back as he opened the door for her.

"It has its moments, but I hope to never return." He stepped in and motioned for Roger to come over.

She wanted to ask him more, but the conversation turned to work for the next hour. The three of them hashed out ideas, went over costs, and by the end of the meeting had finally agreed upon the changes that would be made.

She stood near the back and looked at where her new stage would go. It was a perfect spot. She could just imagine the small tables and chairs around the floor, all facing that direction. The fireplace was off to the side and would provide for a quaint and romantic setting for those close to it. The large windows in front would provide plenty of light during the day, and she planned on having a few rows of lights strung around to help make evenings enjoyable.

Roger had informed her that he'd ordered her bar top and it was ready to install. It was a large chunk of granite that she'd chosen from a local business. She couldn't wait to see it on top of the long bar the men were building. There was plenty of room for the homemade wine racks she'd convinced one of Roger's men, Aaron Miller, to make. She'd known the man since childhood and he made beautiful cabinets and furniture. She had tried to convince him to make her bar stools, but so far he'd been too busy to give her an answer.

Travis had left, saying he had to check in on the theater and the park. She didn't like that he was investing so much time in her project but had to admit that so far, he hadn't done any harm. Then she remembered her bathroom and gasped. Rushing around, she found Roger in the back room and quickly asked him what Travis had changed upstairs.

When he informed her that there were no changes to her apartment, she couldn't help but smile. Maybe he wasn't as big of a jerk as she'd thought.

Travis stood back and looked at the mess that used to be the theater. This project was going to be the death of him, he just knew it.

Holly's place would be finished in the next few months. The park would be finished before that, but the theater project was going to take a full year, if not more. Since Roger was overseeing both of the rebuilds and his time was currently focused on Holly's place, he had to show himself inside. Demolition had already taken place, but where Holly's place now had electric and plumbing and some walls had been put up, the theater was still bare.

When he'd walked in and found no electricity, he should have called it a day, but instead, he'd found a large flashlight and had walked around writing notes until his hand and head hurt from thinking about everything that needed to be done. His father had drawn up plans for both places, and he'd spent a good portion of the evening last night looking them over in his home office. He had to admit that his father had been a genius at architecture. Sure, he'd come up with a few of his own ideas, but his father had a way of putting it all together.

He wondered why his dad hadn't started all this earlier. Then a memory popped into his head of his parents fighting and he knew why. His mother. She'd always opposed him spending his time on projects. Especially after the Mustang incident. He frowned a little, remembering how hurt he and his father had been when his mother had rejected the car and turned her nose up at all the hard work they had done. The car had sat in the garage, untouched, ever since. Even his father wouldn't drive it.

There had been a sour taste in their mouths regarding it, and he wondered why they hadn't just sold it years ago.

It took him almost two hours to go through the old building. When he walked out, he looked down at his dusty clothes and wished desperately for a shower. As he walked the four blocks to the house, he found himself thinking of Holly again. He chuckled every time he thought of her breaking Savannah's nose. He would have paid anything to have been in that restroom when she'd struck the blow. Not that he condoned violence, or that he wanted to see Savannah suffer. He'd dated her frequently enough over the years that he probably knew her better than most people in town did.

Savannah had a soft side but at the drop of a dime, she could turn into the biggest bitch. It was one of the reasons he chose to steer clear of her now. He didn't want to get mixed up in her web again. She still looked great, although he'd noticed that she was a lot heavier than when she'd surprised him and showed up in Vegas. She'd desperately tried to get him to come back to Fairplay, and when he'd been determined not to, she'd gotten bored and had left.

He stepped through the back door and toed off his shoes. When he thought about heading upstairs to shower, he cringed. He hated showering in his parents' shower, but his bathroom had been painted a pale pink, and he hated going into it. It reminded him of Pepto Bismol. There was a list of things that needed to be done to the old place before he could put it on the market; he just wished they were done already.

Stripping off his shirt and pants, he walked back outside and hit the switch to the pool cover. He smiled when he saw the crystal-clear water and jumped right into the pool in his boxers.

He swam a few laps, cooling off in the water, then flipped over and floated as he watched the colors of the sunset from above his head. He'd missed the quiet of living in the country. Maybe that's why he'd thought about staying in Montana. He'd gone up there earlier this month for a few fights and, after winning them all, Randy had booked more in Billings and he hadn't complained. It was a hundred times better than being stuck in Vegas. Especially since he'd gone clean shortly after arriving in town.

He shook his head remembering how he'd cleaned up, thankful for the man who had not only saved him from a lifetime in prison but had helped mold him into what he was today.

When he opened his eyes, he saw Holly standing next to the edge of the pool, bathing suit on and towel in her hand. "I…I didn't know you were going for a swim. I'll come back later." She turned to go.

"Why?" He started treading water. "It's a big pool." He nodded to the water. He felt himself stir at the sight of her in the small red suit.

She bit her bottom lip and then turned to set her towel down on one of the lawn chairs that sat around the pool. When she turned around, he noticed the small tattoo above her hip. He couldn't help but smile at the small pair of boxing gloves with a pink rose above them.

"For your father?" He nodded to the tattoo. She turned and glanced back, like she'd forgotten it was back there, then nodded.

"What about yours?" She held onto the railing and

stepped slowly into the water. His mouth went dry as he watched her nipples pucker as the cold water hit her skin.

"Mine?" he asked after a moment. He'd forgotten what they were talking about. His eyes refused to move away from the perfect breasts.

"Your tattoos? You have a few of them." She nodded to his arms and chest.

He looked down at his arms and chest. "Some of them I got when I was young and stupid." He looked at the dark design around his left shoulder that held no meaning other than the desire to spend his parents' money and piss his mom off. Then he looked just below it and frowned. "Other ones remind me of what not to do in life. Of where I've been and a promise to never go there again."

"I like the wings." He looked up as she nodded to his chest. She was standing just a few feet away from him now in the shallow water.

"Freedom," he said, not focusing on the conversation.

"From?" She moved closer.

"Here," he blurted out, not paying attention.

"Was it that bad? Being here?"

He nodded. "Wouldn't you feel the same after what happened?"

She shrugged her shoulders, and he watched the water play over her soft skin. He wanted to reach out and touch it, to make sure it was as soft as it looked.

"I guess. It must have been hard," she said, looking down at his chest, avoiding his eyes.

He hadn't realized he'd moved closer until he felt her leg brush up against his. She jolted a little and tried to move back, but he reached out and took hold of her waist under the water. Her skin felt like silk in his hands.

Without thinking, he pulled her closer until she was a breath away. The night colors caused her red hair to look like it was glowing. He'd never seen anything like it before. Her skin looked so soft and he wanted to touch it.

"Travis?" she said, just before wrapping her arms around his neck and kissing him. He couldn't have stopped himself if he'd tried. His hands moved over her skin and he enjoyed the feel of her, the softness of her skin. When her body brushed up against his, he moaned and pulled her closer, rubbing himself up against her, wanting more.

He'd denied himself for too long. Years he'd gone without. Now he didn't want to deny his starving body the feel of a soft woman. Why would he when she was wrapping her legs around his hips, pressing her core up against his desire.

When he pulled back and looked at her, he realized his breath was coming out in gasps. He tried to steady and level it, but then he noticed that her breath was coming quickly too.

"I'm sorry," she said, resting her forehead on his. Her eyes were closed, and he felt her arms relax around him.

"For?" He smiled a little when she shook her head.

"I guess nothing." She laughed a little and looked at him nervously. "It's just been a while."

He smiled. "For me as well, but you don't see me apologizing."

She smiled. "This is a very bad idea," she said, running her hands over his shoulders.

"Probably," he agreed, not wanting to make the next move. He had a plan and falling for a small-town bookstore owner wasn't part of it. But he didn't see any reason why he couldn't entertain himself while he was here. The chances of him actually falling for a woman like Holly were slim, so he saw no harm in going for it.

"Then why can't my mind seem to stop my body?" She moved her hips, sending a wave of pleasure to his groin. He closed his eyes and thrust back and enjoyed the small sound she made.

"Don't stop it," he said, taking her mouth. This time he gave in to the urgency he felt. He let his hands travel over her body, enjoying the feel of her nipples puckering under his fingertips. When she moaned and threw her head back, he pulled her suit aside and hoisted her above the water, placing his mouth to the tender peak. She gasped and gripped his hair tighter.

Then he pushed her swimsuit bottom down those sexy legs of hers and pushed a finger gently into her heat. He moaned when he felt her convulse around it as she screamed out. He backed her up until he could hoist her up on the side of the pool and then he held her legs wide as he knelt between her spread legs.

When he touched his tongue to the sensitive skin where his fingers had just been, she screamed again and gripped his hair tightly. He didn't mind because her taste had flooded all of his senses. She tasted better than he'd imagined. Her hips rocked against his mouth until he tasted her burst onto his tongue.

Then he jumped out of the pool and picked her up, carrying her up the outside stairs into what used to be his apartment.

"Damn," he said, looking around. Her eyes flew open.

"What?" She looked around while trying to cover herself with her hands.

He would have chuckled, but he was too horny.

"I forgot that none of my stuff is in here. Do you have protection?" He looked around, trying to remember if he had any rubbers in his bag.

She giggled and nodded. "Top drawer next to the bed."

"Good girl." He carried her into the back room. When he laid her down on the bed, he reached over and took out a silver package, then moved her legs wider and settled between them again. "You taste like sugar." He smiled, then used his tongue and licked her lower lips. "Sweet as sugar." She smiled and wrapped her legs around his shoulders. "You have a way about you." Her eyes closed as she leaned back and enjoyed him.

When he slid a finger into her, her back arched off the mattress and he felt her legs grow tighter around his shoulders.

"You like that?" He smiled when she moaned and nodded. "You have the most beautiful pussy."

He didn't know if it was the three-year hiatus talking or the fact that he'd never seen anything as perfect as she was.

When he finally moved up and positioned himself right outside of her heat, he felt his arms shake, his body shake with anticipation. He wanted the moment to last but knew that too soon he'd be spent. He wasn't usually quick; he'd pleased a lot of women in the past. But the last few people he'd slept with had complained that he was a selfish lover. Both Alexis and Savannah had said so.

He felt a shiver of nerves run through him and wanted to hold out as long as he could. For himself and for her. When he slid into her, he closed his eyes and tried hard to focus on making the feeling last. Then she moved, and he couldn't stop his hips from flexing, over and over again.

She wrapped her legs around his hips, and her nails dug into his shoulders. He looked down at her and saw her blue eyes turn darker. Her lips were swollen slightly and when he leaned down and kissed them, he realized she was on the verge of coming. He grabbed her bent leg and hoisted it up to his chest, then reached down and touched her slightly and watched the most beautiful thing he'd seen in years. Her skin flushed, she bit her swollen bottom lip, and she moaned with pleasure. Her wet hair was fanned out over the pillow and all he could think about doing was making her come again and again.

He began to move faster and faster and felt himself building up, but he wanted to wait. Wait until she could come with him this time.

"Please," she begged.

"What?" he groaned. "Tell me." He used his hips and held her leg close to his chest, gripping her sweet ass in his hand. His nails dig into the soft skin, and he wished he could bury his face into the softness.

"Travis, come with me." She shook her head back and forth, and he realized she was on the edge once more. This time he knew he would go with her. Leaning down, he kissed her so deeply that he felt his heart skip as he let himself go completely for the first time in his life.

*H*olly lay there and listened to their breathing. What had she done? She'd just had wild, crazy sex with one of the baddest boys in Texas. That's what! Everyone in Fairplay—hell, in the county— knew what Travis Nolan was. He was no good. Never would be. His father had bailed him out of jail more times than anyone could count.

He was trouble and she'd just had the best sex she'd ever had in her twenty-five years with him. And, God help her, she wanted to do it again. She peeked open one of her eyes and tried to see, but the sun had set and it was now too dark in the room to see anything. Opening both of her eyes, she turned her head and tried to make out his shape.

"I guess you're going to kick me out now," he said, chuckling a little.

"No, I wasn't going to." She turned and leaned up on her elbow towards him. "Why? Get kicked out of beds a lot?"

He chuckled again. "Not lately."

She ran her fingers over the muscles in his chest. He had not been this built the last time she'd seen him. Actually, she remembered thinking that he'd gained a beer belly and love handles the last time she saw him, years ago.

"Why did you choose cage fighting?" she asked, absentmindedly.

"It chose me." He took her hand in his and intertwined their fingers.

"Oh?" She liked the feeling of his fingers in hers.

"I was in Vegas all of three months when I ran out of money. I didn't want to write home and ask for more." He shrugged his shoulders and sighed. "I guess I was hoping I could make it on my own. I ended up trying to sell my truck to some sleazeball who decided he'd rather take it than pay for it. I kicked his ass and then his buddy, a three-hundred-pound Mexican, jumped out of his car. I thought I was dead. Instead, the man handed me a business card and invited me to my first underground match. Randy put up the money for me to enter the match, paid for my rent for the rest of the month, and told me that if I won, he'd pay my rent for the rest of the year along with a big bonus. I won the first match and got sucked in. He bought me a membership to a local gym and…" He closed his eyes and she could see in the darkness that he was tense about the memory. "The rest is history."

"Do you enjoy it?"

His eyes opened, and he looked at her. She wished for the light, so she could see what he was feeling. "I used to, I guess, for a time. Fighting helped clean up my life. But now I feel like it's keeping me down."

"What do you mean?"

"I have obligations that I can't escape." He sat up and

reached for the light. The soft glow filled the room and he stood up. There were more tattoos on his back, smaller but still as impressive as the ones on his chest. She felt she could spend hours exploring them, running her fingers over each line, each dip in muscle. "I have to go back to Vegas next week. Just for a few days." He ran his hands through his hair, messing the locks up, causing them to stand straight up.

"Can I come with you?" She sat up, pulling the sheet over herself.

He was in the process of pulling on his damp boxers, but stopped and looked up at her. "Why?"

She shrugged and smiled. "To watch you fight."

He shook his head. "You don't belong at an illegal cage fight."

"And you do?" she said, scooting to the edge of the bed.

He grunted and yanked up his boxers. "Goodnight." He started walking towards the door.

"Travis?" She waited until he stopped and looked back at her. "Stay."

For a moment it looked as if he wanted to, but then he shook his head and walked out without another word. She looked at the closed door for a while then sighed and leaned against the headboard.

She'd asked for trouble. After all, he'd made no commitments. Hadn't even hinted at them. No doubt she'd just had her very first one-night stand.

Then she realized how big of a fool she'd made of herself. Why had she asked to go with him? It was obvious he didn't want a relationship. And here she was practically begging to go to Vegas with him next week.

Getting up, she walked into the bathroom and decided what she needed was a long hot shower to get clean. She stood under the spray and dreamed of the day that she could take a long bath in her new apartment. Maybe then she could wash off the gross feeling that she had, knowing she'd just been used. Even worse, she'd used him right back. Would that feeling ever go away? She began to hate him for coming back, for being so damn sexy. And for tricking her into believing he had changed somehow.

When she walked back out, she was shocked to see Savannah laying down in her bed, clothed in only a tiny pink nighty.

"What the hell?" She sat up and covered herself with Holly's sheets.

Holly laughed and wrapped her robe around herself tighter.

"Where's Travis?" Savannah looked off towards the bathroom, no doubt expecting Travis to walk out half-naked.

"You're in the wrong house," she said dryly. "He's staying in the main house. I live here temporarily." She tossed Savannah her coat, which was thrown over the chair. Then Holly walked towards the front door. "I'm sure he'll be excited to see you." She held the door open as Savannah tied the long coat around her large form.

When Holly shut the door behind her, she forced herself not to look out the window and see if Travis let her in. Instead, she stood with her back to the door and listened as closely as she could. When she didn't hear anything, she walked back into the bedroom and desperately tried not to cry.

She sat on the edge of the bed, and suddenly something

flashed in her head. Rushing to the phone, she picked it up and dialed Melissa's number.

"Hello?" Her friend sounded tired.

"I'm sorry." She glanced at the clock and realized it was past ten at night. She knew that Melissa worked the early shift at the health clinic and most nights was in bed by eight. "I'm sorry," she said again.

"You've already said that. Spill. What's going on that you would call me this late?" Her friend knew her too well.

"Savannah's pregnant."

"What?" Melissa yawned. "You're crazy."

"No, I'm not. Listen. She was just here at my apartment and I saw it for myself."

"How?"

"She was wearing a small teddy."

"What?" She could tell she had Melissa's full attention now. "What was Savannah Douglas doing in your apartment wearing a teddy?"

"What's going on?" she heard Melissa's fiancé, Reece, say in the background.

"Holly claims that Savannah was just in her apartment wearing nothing but a teddy and that she's pregnant."

"Holly's pregnant?" Reece asked, and Holly could hear that he was half-asleep. She tried not to chuckle.

"No, Savannah. Never mind. I'll tell you after I know everything." Melissa turned her attention back to her. "Okay, spill."

"Well, I had just gotten out of the shower, because…" She stopped herself from telling her friend that she'd just made the worst mistake of her life, so she coughed to cover it up. "Anyway, when I came out of the bathroom, there she was, spread out on my bed, wearing nothing but a small—very small—pink teddy. I could see she'd gained some weight but thought nothing of it until after I ushered her out. Then my mind kind of snapped back, and I realized that what I had seen wasn't fat, it was a baby bump."

Then her mind and heart did a giant jump. So much so that she started hyperventilating. If Savannah was pregnant, there was a good chance that Travis was the father. And she'd just had wild, crazy sex with Travis, in this bed. She stood up quickly and glared at the bed, at the sheets. She felt her head spin again.

"Holly!" She realized a moment later that Melissa was screaming into her ear. "Holly, are you okay? Don't make me go over there. Answer me!"

"I'm here." Her voice sounded so far away, she swallowed a few times to try and come back to the present. "Listen, anyway, let's meet for lunch," she said absently. "I'll let you go. Night." She hung up and threw herself back on the bed and cried until she fell asleep.

Travis stepped out of his parents' bathroom and almost fell on his ass. Savannah lay across his parents' bed in nothing more than a pink strip of silk. Her long blonde hair was spread out over his grandmother's handmade quilt. Her manicured fingernails ran up and down the sides of her thighs, which he noticed were a lot larger than they used to be. Even if he hadn't just released his pent-up sexual tension with Holly, he still wouldn't have been excited at the sight of her.

"How did you get in here?" He wrapped the towel tighter around his waist and reached for her arm.

"Oh, come on now. You know I still have a key from when I used to sneak up here," she purred. She gasped when he tugged on her arm and pulled her up to stand next to him.

"Get out," he growled as he started walking towards the hallway.

"How dare you." She jerked her arm away from him. "You never complained before." She ran her fingers up his chest and leaned her breasts against his bare chest. "Besides, I've no doubt you're as bored as I am in this town." She smiled and ran her finger up and pinched his nipple between her nails. "Maybe we can be bored together."

"Out." He jerked her arm away from his chest. "I don't want to play your games anymore." He started walking towards the door but stopped when he noticed her jacket was thrown over his father's reading chair. Tossing it to her, he waited until she tied it around her rather large belly.

"Really, Travis," she said, pulling out a cigarette and lighting it right there in his parents' house. His folks had never allowed him to smoke inside the house, one of the main reasons he'd moved into the apartment above the garage. He used to smoke a pack a day, and he wasn't going to have his folks tell him he couldn't do it inside his own place. She blew the smoke towards his face and he cringed. Gone was the desire, when he smelled smoke, to pick it up again.

He reached over and took the cigarette from her, then walked into the bathroom, tossed it in the sink, and flipped on the faucet.

"Well, really!" she exclaimed. "How dare you treat me like this?" She crossed her arms over her chest and pouted, a move he'd seen a million times.

"You shouldn't be smoking in your condition." Her eyebrows shot up. "You can probably hide it from the town, but not me, not when I just saw you wearing hardly anything." He nodded to the large coat that covered her belly now. "Grow up." He took her hand. "Just do it somewhere else." He walked her to the hallway and started going down the stairs. She faked tripping, but he was ready for it.

When they'd been dating, she had always faked injuries to make him feel like he'd abused her. His hand tightened on her arm and he held her steady.

"Stop it, you could hurt the baby." He cussed when she tried to push his hand away. "Savannah, stop it." He jerked her arm until she walked down the stairs without tripping.

"Let go of me," she shouted.

"Go home." He dropped his hand and opened the front door.

"I hate you," she screamed.

"Good, now go home." He crossed his arms over his chest and waited.

She walked up to him and slapped him in the face. "How dare you treat me like this? The mother of your child." She pouted and big fat tears started falling from her eyes.

"Nice try." He smiled a little. "Try barking up someone else's tree."

"Are you calling me a liar?" She pushed her face into his and he wondered why he'd ever fallen for her games.

He chuckled and then nodded. "I suppose I am. If you

go around claiming that the child is mine, I'll demand a test, which will prove that it's not."

Her bottom lip pushed out and she looked up at him, then her face softened and her voice purred again. "It happened when I was visiting you. It could be yours."

He shook his head no. "We haven't been together in four years, since before…" He stopped himself from saying before his mother had almost killed a man. Instead, he shook his head again. "It's not mine."

She blinked a few times and then started running her fingers over his chest again. "If you want, it can be yours. Ours."

He took her hands and pushed her away. "Not interested." He stepped back. "Goodnight, Savannah."

He watched anger cross her face again. Then she walked up and punched him in the jaw. There wasn't enough power behind it to do much damage, but it caused his head to hit the door behind him. His ears started ringing as she yelled and cussed at him. He waited until she was done, then took her arm again and stepped outside on the front porch and then back in the house. Without a word, he shut her outside.

He listened for a while as she pounded on the door, cussing at him, threatening him with everything from telling everyone that he'd raped her, to saying he'd beaten her and denied that the baby was his. He was just thankful that he could say definitely that the kid wasn't his. He leaned his head against the door and cringed. There was a large knot on the back of it and when he reached back and touched it, he hissed with pain.

Damn, now he was going to have to change the locks.

"It's that slut, isn't it?" she screamed, causing his mind

to sharpen back to what she was screaming. "That slut living in our old apartment."

At first, he didn't know what she was talking about. What apartment? They had never lived together. Then he remembered Holly and he swung open the door.

"Leave Holly out of this."

Savannah's eyebrows shot up. "So, this *is* about her." She crossed her arms over her chest and chuckled. The sound caused his skin to crawl.

"No, just leave her alone. She's just renting the apartment." He moved to shut the door again.

"Well, that's not what she told me when I was up there earlier."

He stopped and yanked open the door again. "You're lying."

"Oh?" She raised her eyebrows again. "She told me all about it. I thought you were staying at your place but found out when she came out of the shower. Now I know. I'm not stupid you know." She yelled the last part.

"Go home." He slammed the door in her face and heard her kick the locked door and scream. Then he heard her Jeep peel out of the driveway. He listened for a while, making sure she was gone, and then he walked to the back of the house and looked towards the apartment.

Holly's light was still on, making him wonder if she'd heard everything that had just gone on. For some reason, he didn't want Savannah and her craziness to touch Holly.

CHAPTER 6

The next morning Holly stood in her store and smiled. The bar top had arrived. The thing weighed a ton, and she stood back and watched as the men lowered it in place with two forklifts.

They drilled and screwed large bolts into place until it was secure. Then Holly rushed over and tested it for herself. It was solid. She smiled over at Roger.

"Perfect."

"It does look good." He stood back and smiled at her. "I didn't think the look would work, but now I can see what you had in mind."

She nodded. "I'm still trying to convince Aaron to make my bar stools." She looked out of the side of her eyes towards Roger.

He ran his hand over his two-day-old beard. "Maybe I can give him some time off so he can focus on the stools."

"Oh!" She rushed over and hugged him.

"But it will have to be after we're done here. When we start working on the theater," he warned her.

65

"I'll take it." She smiled and then leaned up and placed a kiss on his rough face.

"Am I interrupting?" Travis said from the doorway.

She looked over and smiled at him. She wasn't going to let him or what they had done last night ruin her good mood. Her bar top was in, and she was going to get her unique bar stools. Nothing was going to dampen her mood. Not even Travis and the possibility of him being back with Savannah. Or the possibility of them being a family very soon.

"I have my bar top." She waved her hand towards the bar and smiled, even more, when she looked over and saw how beautiful it was.

"Looks good." He walked over and inspected it, testing his weight on the edge to make sure it didn't move. "Solid work." He nodded towards Roger, who nodded back then quickly disappeared. The men were now pounding away upstairs, putting in her closet and kitchen area.

"It's really coming together." She stood behind the bar and imagined serving customers. In her mind, she envisioned the wall coverings, the lighting, even some of the local artwork she planned on hanging up.

"Listen." He stepped closer to her. "I wanted to apologize for last night."

Her heart dropped in her chest and she tried everything she could to not let the disappointment show on her face. "You don't need to apologize." She turned to go, but he stopped her with a hand on her shoulder.

"I do. Savannah's behavior was unacceptable."

She couldn't stop her eyebrows from rising in question.

"You did hear the yelling, right?"

She shook her head no.

"Oh." He sighed and closed his eyes.

"Yelling?" She stepped closer. "Did you two fight?"

A burst of laughter escaped him. "Let's go outside." He took her hand in his and walked with her to the small patio area. She sat down on the bench and watched him pace.

"She actually broke into my place and lay on my parents' bed. I guess she expected to pick up where we left off years ago." He shook his head and turned towards her. "The fact that she was dishonoring my grandmother's quilt was disturbing enough, but then I noticed that she is pregnant." He laughed again. "She actually tried to pawn it off as mine." He shook his head.

"Isn't it?" she broke in and instantly wished she hadn't. He looked down at her and something crossed his eyes. Was it sadness or was he just tired? "I'm sorry, it's just that she said…"

"I know what she said." He turned away from her and kicked a stone by his foot. "I'm sure she said a lot of things. None of them were true." He turned back towards her. "Believe me, I wouldn't have done what we did…" He ran his hands through his hair, messing it up. "If there was a chance that the kid was mine."

She nodded and stood up. "I believe you."

He looked at her like she'd just slapped him. "You do?"

She nodded. "Sure. Savannah lies." She waved her hand. "No one in town believes a word she says."

He looked surprised and blinked a few times. "I can remember a time when the same could be said about me."

She nodded. "When your mother was on her rampage."

He frowned at her. "Some people still blame me."

"Why? Why would they? You had nothing to do with it."

He crossed his arms over his chest. "I cheated on Alex, my fiancée at the time."

"Lots of people cheat. That doesn't give their parents' permission to go off half-cocked. Nor does it make it your fault."

He blinked a few times like he was thinking about it, then he nodded. "I suppose you're right."

She chuckled. "Of course, I'm right."

"Why did you ask to go to Vegas with me?"

Now it was her turn to be surprised. "I told you, I've never been to Vegas."

"Is that all?" He stepped closer.

She nodded, feeling his heat jump across the small space towards her.

"No other reason?" He stopped less than a foot from her.

She shook her head no, unable to speak.

"What would you say if I told you that the only reason I didn't want you to come was that I was embarrassed."

"Why?" She frowned again, finding her voice.

He shook his head and closed his eyes. "The life I chose. What I do."

"Cage fighting? I've watched it on TV. It looks pretty intense."

"It is." He frowned. "Even more so since it's all underground."

"You mean illegal?" He nodded. "But it's not banned in the States."

"It's regulated. This one's not."

"It can't be too different." She held her breath when he reached out and brushed her hair away from her face.

"If you come with me, I wouldn't want you to go to the fight."

She frowned. "Why not?"

He shook his head. "Because. Promise me that you wouldn't ask to go."

She looked up into his dark eyes and saw sadness there. "I promise."

When he smiled, she felt her breath knocked from her chest. It was the first time she'd seen his lips curl up into a genuine smile. His dark eyes lightened. He looked handsome when he was brooding, but when he was happy, he looked damn sexy.

"We leave Monday morning." He leaned down and placed a soft kiss on her lips. "I have a meeting with Roger in an hour. We're supposed to go to the theater and go over some things. But I'd like to have dinner with you later."

She smiled and nodded. "I'd like that. I can cook something."

His eyebrows shot up. "Your place then?"

When she nodded again, he leaned down and this time the kiss was slow and sent warm sparks shooting out through her toes.

She spent the next half an hour cleaning every inch of her bar top. When she looked down at her watch, she realized she was going to be late for her lunch with Melissa and had to jog across the street to meet her friend.

"I'm sorry." She hugged her friend and then sat down. "I got sidetracked admiring my bar top and lost track of time."

"Oh, it came?" Missy asked, looking over her menu.

"Yes, they just installed it an hour ago." She sighed and rested her chin on her hands. "It looks wonderful."

"I can't wait to see it. Maybe I can stop by after work."

She shook her head. "Can't. I have a date."

Missy's eyebrows shot up. "Date? Do you have a date? With who?"

She leaned forward and whispered, "Travis Nolan."

"What?" Missy's voice rose over the noise in the diner, causing a few people to glance in their direction.

Holly smiled and nodded. "I have so much to tell you." She leaned forward and started at the beginning.

By the time their plates were empty, Melissa was smiling. "It sure sounds like he's changed. I always knew he'd grow up sooner or later. Or," she frowned, "he would end up dead, shot by the husband of the woman he'd just had an affair with."

Holly nodded. "I know." She shook her head. "Honestly, I can't even see that person in him anymore."

Melissa sighed. "People can change. Look at Reece. Before he came back to town, he was traveling with the rodeo and"—she leaned forward and whispered—"sleeping with anyone and everyone he could."

Holly shook her head. "I can't imagine Reece doing anything like that."

"I know." Missy sighed. "He's all mine now."

"You're lucky, both of you."

"Can you believe only four more months and we'll be married?" She frowned a little. "We had hoped that Ryan would be there. You know, Reece's twin brother? Reece hasn't seen him since shortly before their father had died. He has no idea where he is. We've hired an old friend of my dad's to see if he could locate him, but so far we haven't heard anything back."

"I'm sure you'll find him in time." Holly reached across the table and held her friend's hand.

"So," Missy said, shaking her head. "Tell me all about Savannah. How far along do you think she is?"

"I was hoping you'd know. Hasn't she been coming into the clinic for checkups?"

Missy shook her head and frowned. "Maybe she's going into Tyler and seeing a doctor there?"

"I hope. Travis said she was still smoking."

"What?" Missy almost stood up. "How stupid can you get?"

"I know."

"Someone has to stop her."

Holly almost laughed. "I tried that once, remember? I almost ended up in jail."

Missy sat quietly for a moment. "I wonder if her parents know."

"I doubt it." Then something came to mind. "Oh my God! I broke her nose."

Missy looked at her. "I know. I was there.

"No, I mean, I broke her nose and she was pregnant at the time."

"Oh." Missy frowned. "A broken nose wouldn't have hurt the baby."

"Still." She knew her friend was just trying to reassure her, but it didn't negate the fact that she'd hit a pregnant woman.

"Holly," Melissa said reaching across the table and taking her hand, "you didn't know. You didn't hurt the baby more than one puff of a cigarette is doing to it."

"You're right. She has to be stopped. What's your plan?"

"How about an intervention?"

Holly shook her head. "She wouldn't listen to us. She hates us."

"Right." Missy tapped her finger to her chin and smiled. "I've got it. Sheriff Miller."

"What's the sheriff got to do with it?"

"He's friends with her parents. If he lets it slip that he saw her smoking, and they know about her pregnancy..."

She smiled. "I like where you're going with this, but we have to make sure they know she's pregnant."

"Who's pregnant?" Alex stood next to their table, a sleeping little girl in her arms. Her daughter's hair was as pale as hers and even though she had the blue eyes of her daddy, the girl was a spitting image of her mama.

"There's my niece." Missy stood and reached for the sleepy girl. Alex gladly handed over the two-year-old.

"She's gotten so big. I almost forget how heavy she is until I hand her over," Alex said, sitting down and sighing. "Now, tell me who's pregnant."

"Savannah Douglas."

Alex laughed. "Everyone knows that. All you have to do is look at her to know it."

"Everyone?" Missy asked, brushing a blonde strand of hair from her niece's hair.

"Sure, I knew it the night you punched her in the face." She nodded to Holly. "I guess since you two haven't been pregnant before, you wouldn't have picked up on the signs." She smiled. "Like, you probably don't know that I'm three months along now."

"What?" Missy almost woke the sleeping Laura in her arms. "You're pregnant now?" she whispered.

Alex smiled and nodded. "A little over three months."

"Why didn't you tell me sooner?" Missy asked.

"We wanted to wait until we knew the sex." She picked up a menu and looked down at it.

"Alex, if you don't tell me the sex right now, I'm going to…"

Alex smiled over at her sister-in-law. "We're having a boy."

"Woohoo!" Missy said, this time waking up the sleeping girl in her arms. "Oh, baby, I'm sorry." She rubbed the little girl's hair and soothed her back to sleep as they all smiled.

CHAPTER 7

*T*ravis was dirty again. Why did it seem that every time he stepped foot in the old theater, he walked out looking like he'd crawled through the fields? He looked at his watch and realized he was going to be late for dinner at Holly's if he ran up and showered, so he decided to jump into the pool instead. When he opened the back gate, Holly was sitting by the pool in a light blue sundress. She had decorated the picnic table, and he noticed that it was filled with food and the grill was going and wonderful smells were coming from it. There were candles and tiki lamps placed around the yard, lighting up the area. He'd never seen the place look better.

"Hi." She smiled. "I thought we'd eat out here."

"Sounds wonderful. I'll just run up and shower." He looked down at his clothes.

"You can take a dip." She nodded to the opened pool. "I'll join you. The brisket won't be ready for a while yet." She stood up and his mouth went dry as she pulled the blue cotton over her head. She was wearing a white suit this time and when she stepped into the water, the light material became transparent.

He stripped his clothes off quickly, keeping his eyes locked on her. He was thankful he'd stopped by the drug store and had purchased a box of condoms. Tossing one by the side of the pool, he jumped in next to her, causing her to laugh.

"Smooth," she said, swimming over to him. "How did your meeting go?"

He shook his head. "I don't want to talk about meetings when you're standing before me dressed like that." He nodded to her swim top. It was so see-through, he could see her nipples pucker under his watchful eyes. "Come here." He reached for her and got hold of her ankle and playfully pulled her to him.

She laughed until his hands touched her skin until his mouth covered hers in heat. He couldn't stop the flood of desire he felt when he looked at her. He had allowed the floodgates to open and now there was no stopping his desires.

Her hands raked over his body as his rushed to push the small white material from her. Finally, when they were both freed, he kicked a few times until they were by the side of the pool. He put on the condom quickly then pushed her back up against the wall and slid into her in one quick motion.

She arched and cried out in delight, holding onto him tightly until he felt her convulse around him, then he picked her up and carried her to a recliner and laid her down. When he covered her, she moaned and wrapped her arms around him and kissed him until he felt himself lose the last thread of restraint he'd had.

"I hadn't planned this, you know." She chuckled into his shoulder.

"Why on earth not?" He smiled and placed a kiss on her shoulder.

"Well, maybe I had hoped to wait until after we had eaten." She smiled. "Oh!" She sat up, pushing on his shoulder until he moved over. "My brisket."

She rushed across the backyard bare naked and pulled the cooked meat from the grill.

"Whew, saved it." She turned, and he couldn't stop himself from laughing. She was wearing two oven mitts and nothing else, and she looked damn sexy.

Holly sat across from Travis in her blue sundress. She hadn't bothered putting her wet swimsuit back on since he'd just pulled on his jeans. They ate her dinner outside on the patio and when the sun went down, she poured some cold iced tea from the small fridge by the grill, and they sat and talked and ate some of the cranberry bread she'd baked.

She kept telling herself not to put too much stock into their relationship, but the fact was that the more time she spent with him, the more she enjoyed his companionship more the more time she spent with him. He talked about some of the stupid stuff he had done growing up. About all the times his friends had gotten him in trouble, or the other way around.

"It doesn't sound like Corey and Billy have changed much. Do you know I saw them car surfing down Main Street, bare-ass naked, just last month?"

He chuckled and shook his head. "They're either going to kill themselves or someone will do it for them."

"You know; we could have said the same about you a few years ago." She took a sip of her drink.

He nodded. "I know." He frowned and then set his drink down, stood, and then started pacing. "I was an alcoholic, a drug addict, and a fool." He shook his head. "I was heading down the same path that Billy and Corey are still going down." He stopped and looked down at her. She set her tea down and watched him, waiting. "I went to Vegas thinking I'd get rich by gambling. I was pretty good at cards. I thought I could take care of myself." He shook his head. "Within the first week I ended up in jail with a DUI." He shook his head. "They strip search you when you get there, you know." He took a deep breath. "I had a few ounces of coke on me." He closed his eyes, remembering. "I was looking at ten to twenty years in prison, and my father wasn't there to bail me out this time. But then something happened. The officer on duty was a little older than my father. Anyway, I guess he saw me sweat, or maybe he just took pity on me. He held the bag of coke in his hands, looked over at me, and said, 'We'll just flush this.' Then he flushed it down the toilet without another word." Travis sat in the chair next to her and looked down at his hands. "I never drank, smoked, or did drugs after that. Not after being given a second chance at life. To be honest, I haven't had the desire to do any of those things again." He shook his head and ran his hands through his hair. "It's funny, my old man used to bail me out like that all the time, but nothing had ever scared me before or meant more to me than having that man give me a second chance that night."

"What did you do?"

"Well, since I lost my license that day and had a pile of legal bills, I tried to sell my truck and ran into Randy." He sighed and leaned back in his chair.

"I'm sorry." She reached over and took his hands. "It sounds like you had a guardian angel."

He looked up at her. "It's funny how you can turn something negative into something else."

She smiled. "My father died when I was young, so I barely remember him, but if I close my eyes"—she did now, and the image came to her like it always did when she thought of her dad— "I can picture him teaching me how to fight. He has a big smile on his face and he is laughing." She opened her eyes. "But when I open them and think of him, I can only remember the day he died and the heartache he left."

"How did he die?"

She closed her eyes and brought back the good memory of her dad. "He hung himself in my closet. I found him when I went to get my boxing gloves for practice."

"I'm sorry." He squeezed her hands gently.

She shook her head. "They claimed it was PTSD. But I remember him as happy and always laughing." She hadn't realized a tear had slipped down her cheek until he reached over and wiped it away with a fingertip. She took a deep breath. "Well, enough of that. What do you say to another swim?" She stood up and he followed, but then he pulled her into his arms and gently kissed her.

Instantly, she felt heat spread throughout her.

"Travis?" She tried to control what was inside her. She watched him shake his head.

"I'd rather go upstairs." He started walking them towards the stairs and she followed.

When they reached her room, he slowly peeled her dress off again and then stood back and looked at her.

"Beautiful," he whispered before reaching out and touching her gently with the back of his hand. He ran his fingers slowly over her skin, sending shivers down her spine. She closed her eyes and rolled her head backward, enjoying the feel of him touching her.

"Travis—" She couldn't voice her desires, so instead she opened her eyes and pushed him backward until he fell on the bed. Then she slowly pulled his jeans from him, unbuttoning them, slowly unzipping them, and peeling them from his hips. When she leaned down and kissed the sexy muscles that played on his stomach, his hands went to her hair.

She pulled his jeans off completely and spent her time pleasing him with her mouth until he begged for her. Sliding up his body, she let every part of her touch him until she straddled his hips and looked down at him. He was beautiful. His dark eyes looked at her full of desire and need.

When he took her hips into his hands and hoisted her up until she could slide down on his full length, she smiled and moaned with delight. He filled her so completely, she felt like she might burst at first contact.

When she started to move, she reached down and rested her palms on his chest and felt his heart skip with hers. The faster she moved on him, the quicker she felt herself build up. She cried out his name as lights exploded behind her eyes, and then she rested her head against his chest. He held her for a moment, and then he reversed their positions as he continued the smooth motion, and she felt herself building again. She wrapped her legs around his hips, trying to hold him as tightly as she could as his hands moved slowly over her body. His lips were on her nipples, gently sucking when she fell again. This time he stilled with her and moaned her name with his release.

When he started to move, she held him tight. "No, don't go just yet," she said against his cool skin.

He chuckled. "I'm just going to roll off you. I must be squashing you."

She shook her head. "It feels good. You feel good." She ran her hands over his back, playing with the muscles she felt in his shoulders, his lower back.

He groaned. "Holly, you're killing me here."

She smiled, knowing she could excite him by just touching him. She already felt him hardening inside her again and wanted to explore even more. Her hands ran lower, and she heard him groan as he started to move again.

"I'll get you back for this," he said against her ear softly. "Just wait…"

She didn't have the voice to tell him that she looked forward to it. Instead, she lay back and enjoyed every moment she had with him while she could.

The next morning, she was surprised to roll over and find him still lying next to her, looking at her. "Morning," he said, reaching over and pushing a wayward strand of hair from her face.

"Morning," she smiled. "What are your plans today?"

He frowned. "I have to swing by the park; they're installing the playground today."

"Oh!" She smiled. "That's wonderful." He nodded. "I'd love to swing by and see it after."

"Sure." He rolled over and sat up, stretching his arms over his head. "I need to go work out first." He looked over his shoulder. "If I'm going to win Tuesday, that is." His eyes looked sad all of a sudden.

"If you don't want to fight"—she sat up and hugged her knees— "why don't you call it off?"

He shook his head. "Can't." He got up and started walking to the bathroom.

"Why not?" She followed him.

He turned to her, one hand on the shower door. "Commitments. It's not a pretty world, underground fighting." He shook his head. "You wouldn't understand." He climbed in the shower, and she stood there watching him for a moment. Then she marched over to the shower and opened the door.

"Then tell me. Why can't you call off a fight? Why don't you just quit fighting?"

He looked at her, his head under the spray. "Because I owe Randy money. Lots of money. And until I pay him back every dime, I have to fight." He dumped some shampoo on his head and turned around, dismissing her.

"What about going to the police?" He shook his head no. "They'll probably work with you. I mean, if you turn them all in."

She climbed in the small shower with him.

"Hey!" He stepped back, making room for her. "There isn't enough room in here."

"Sure there is. I'm small enough." She reached up and took some shampoo and started scrubbing her long hair.

He frowned down at her, then reached over and took

over rubbing the soap through her hair. "I'm going to smell like you all day." He leaned forward and sniffed her shampoo.

She smiled. "Then you'll think of me all day."

His frown grew. "Are you always this cheery in the morning?"

She chuckled. "Usually more so. I haven't had my coffee yet. I can't wait until my cappuccino machine is back in business." She moaned thinking of a cup of the wonderful elixir.

"You have a cappuccino machine?"

She nodded. "For the shop."

He groaned. "I'd kill for a good cup."

"I know what you mean. I guess we could go to Mama's before you head over to the park."

He frowned. "Yeah, sometimes her coffee tastes like burnt water."

She laughed. "The food is great though."

He was rubbing his hands over her back as she did the same for him.

"I could eat," he said, looking into her eyes and she knew that the shower was about to get a lot smaller.

CHAPTER 8

The next few days he filled with work and working out. He had to maintain his body if he planned on not getting killed in the ring. He spent hours hitting the bag on the back porch.

Her words played over and over in his head. He knew even if he had the money, Randy would never leave him alone. The amount he owed him kept climbing with every fight and jumped even higher every time he lost. He thought about making a few calls to see if he had any other options. He only had a few days if he was going to change his life forever.

Holly would sit by the pool and watch him hit the bag in the evenings. Other times he'd take off and run through the streets of the small town. He'd forgotten how nice people were in this town. On several occasions, he'd stopped and chatted with someone. So far, no one had even mentioned his mother or what had happened. Instead, they were all curious where he'd been, what he'd done, and what his plans were for the future.

Several people stopped him and talked about the projects his father had started. They also mentioned other projects that they thought should be next. He quickly set them straight that as soon as these commitments were finished, he was leaving town.

He even talked to the only real estate agent in town and had him looking into listing the big house. He agreed to get the place appraised first, but Travis knew that there was a little work that had to be completed before it would sell.

First thing Monday morning, they packed up his small car and headed to the Dallas airport for their flight to Vegas. He wanted to make sure to hit Vegas before Randy sent someone after him. He'd done that before and Travis had ended up with a bruised jaw and ribs.

"I can't believe I'm actually going to fly," Holly said, looking out the small window of the plane.

"You haven't flown anywhere before?" he asked, stowing his small bag overhead.

She shook her head. "No. I've never been outside of Texas before, either." She smiled and looked up at him.

He shook his head and sat next to her. "I thought you said your mother moved to Florida a few years ago."

She nodded. "She grew up there and still has family down there."

"But you've never been down there to visit?"

She shook her head. "I've been busy with the bookstore."

He looked over at her. "Sounds like you need to hire an employee or find another job."

She shook her head. "You know, I used to think about moving out of Fairplay all the time." She sighed and looked out the window again. "But in the last few months, since your father agreed to rebuild the place…" She turned to him again. "I've stopped dreaming about it."

He frowned. "So, your content with living the rest of your life in Fairplay?"

She nodded and smiled. "It's the perfect place to be. The people are wonderful, and I know everyone. I have a successful business and a wonderful place to live. Or I will once it's all done. Why would I want to start all over?" She smiled.

He played her words over in his mind during the flight and by the time they landed in Vegas, he was seriously thinking that he had to show her how great the world was, and he'd start with showing her a wonderful time in Vegas.

They rode the shuttle to the hotel, and he got that old feeling of being watched. He knew that Randy probably had guys looking out for him to see if he'd actually show up. He hated knowing that they would know he hadn't come alone.

When they walked into the hotel, he had to hand it to Randy—the man always booked the best places. Of course, the price always came out of his winnings, but he had never really minded it in the past.

"Oh, my…" She set her small bag down and turned circles in the large room. "There's a pool in the room." She walked towards the small pool that overlooked the city.

"Yeah, I've stayed here a couple times." He walked towards the staircase that led to the bedroom with their bags in his hand.

"You've stayed here before?" She turned and watched him climb the staircase. Then she rushed around the place, checking out everything. There was a small kitchenette, a huge TV room with large circular sofas, and a bedroom that was twice the size of the whole apartment above Travis' garage.

"Why don't we head downstairs and play some slot machines?" he asked after she was done looking around.

"I've never gambled before." She smiled, and he felt her excitement.

"I've always loved it." He shook his head. "But I'm not very lucky." He took her hand as they headed to the elevators. "Maybe you'll be my lucky charm.?"

Less than two hours later, Holly stood with three buckets of coins, smiling at him as he put in his last coin and watched the machine eat it up.

"I guess there's no such thing as luck rubbing off on me." He frowned as her machine spit out another handful of coins.

"Can you believe this?" She gathered up the coins and dumped them into his cup. "Keep going."

He laughed and started putting coins into the machine again. "There ought to be a law against being so lucky." He watched her shove more coins into her machine.

When the lights started flashing and the music played loudly, signaling that she'd hit the jackpot of eight-hundred dollars, he gave up and sat back to watch her.

He'd never seen anyone smile and laugh so much in his life. She genuinely looked like she was having the best time of her life. By the time they cashed in her coins, she had won over a thousand dollars. He'd blown a couple thousand the first week he'd been in Vegas but had never imagined someone would win so much.

"I can't believe how lucky you are," he said, taking her hand as they walked towards the elevators. "What do you say we change and then you take me out for dinner?" He smiled over at her.

She laughed. "Sounds wonderful."

By the time he'd changed into his best shirt and dress pants, he was feeling a little anxious about the fight tomorrow evening. He always got nervous a few days before, but usually spent his time burning it off in the gym. However, this time he was with Holly and wanted to make sure to show her a good time. He didn't know why it was so important to him that she enjoy herself, but it mattered.

His mind flashed to the last time he'd fought Steve Cann, his opponent tomorrow night. It was over a year ago and all he could remember was that he'd barely beaten the man.

He watched Holly walk down the stairs, and his mind blanked. His only thought was of her. She wore a short silver dress with thin straps that held the beaded sash across her breasts. Soft material flowed around her legs with every step. Her tall silver heels sparkled in the dying sunlight that flooded in through the large windows. Her hair was pulled to one side and swept over her shoulder in waves.

He stood without a word and just looked at her as she walked towards him.

"Well?" She bit her bottom lip that was slicked with shiny lip gloss, making him want to kiss them to see if they tasted as good as they looked. When she got close enough, he smelled the sweetness of her perfume, which sent waves of desire rushing through him.

"You look amazing." He took a step towards her and realized he didn't trust himself to touch her. Not yet. So, he tucked his hands into his jacket pockets.

Her smile faltered a little, so he chimed in, "Ready to eat?"

She nodded and followed him out the door. They were silent during the short ride in the elevator. His eyes kept going back to her, watching her move, breath. She was mesmerizing. He reached over and took her hand as the doors opened. She looked up at him and smiled.

They walked two blocks to one of his favorite restaurants and waited to be seated. It took a few minutes, but he knew the wait would be worth it. When they were seated right next to the large windows that overlooked the city, he enjoyed the excitement he saw on her face.

He ordered champagne, and she smiled over at him.

"We have to celebrate your winnings." He took her hand in his.

"I've never had as much fun as I did today."

"You deserved it." He nodded towards the menu. "I can recommend the salmon or the halibut. I haven't tried anything else." He looked down at his menu. "I try not to eat too heavy the night before a fight."

She looked down at her menu. "The steak sounds wonderful."

He chuckled. "I thought you were on a fish only diet?"

She smiled. "What happens in Vegas…"

He chuckled. "If you get it, maybe you can let me have a nibble. I haven't had red meat in months."

"I would have thought that you'd be on a strict diet of red meat and protein."

He shook his head. "I went to a trainer a few years ago and he started me on an almost all vegetarian diet. He said that with my body type, too much protein would slow me down." He tilted his head. "So far it's worked out great for me. Over a hundred wins and only a handful of losses."

She leaned forward. "How can you stand all the pain?" She leaned back and blushed. "I've watched it on television and it looks so painful."

He frowned and nodded. "It is. I guess I push it aside." He thought about his mother and shivered. "I think of something terrible and the pain doesn't seem so bad."

"What would be so bad?" She frowned, looking at him, waiting.

He was spared from answering when the waiter came over and took their order.

"I know I promised not to ask to go tomorrow night, but I was hoping you'd change your mind about letting me cheer you on," she said after the waiter left with their orders.

He shook his head no. "It's no place for you. Besides, I don't want Randy to know about you. He's not what you'd call a good agent."

"From what you've told me about him, he seems more like a pimp than an agent."

"That sounds right. I've tried everything to get out from under him. My inheritance is the one shot I have at paying him off and finally getting free."

"How much do you owe him?"

He looked up at her and sighed. "Fifteen thousand at my last count."

"What?" She almost choked on her champagne. "How did it get to be so much?"

He shrugged. "There's an entrance fee to each fight. The first year he had me fighting a lot and I won some and lost some. He puts me up in the hotels, cars if I need them. He paid for my trainer. I guess it just built up."

"How much do you win each fight?"

"It depends. The most I've won was a little over three grand."

Her chin dropped. "Yet you still owe him fifteen?" He nodded. "Travis, he's ripping you off."

He looked at her. "What do you mean?"

She shook her head. "I've helped my mother at the bookstore since I was thirteen. The first thing she had me doing was balancing the books. I paid the bills, made sure the orders were paid for, and have been responsible for pretty much every dime that has come in or gone out of that place ever since. There is no way you have made several grand each fight and still owe your agent fifteen. How much commission does he take?"

"Thirty-five percent."

She coughed. "What?"

He was beginning to feel stupid. He knew he wasn't good at math. Hell, he'd flunked algebra twice in high school. He'd trusted Randy, especially in the beginning, but over the last few years, he'd begun to doubt him. Especially after the man had started charging him for things he hadn't agreed to.

"I've known for a while that he was ripping me off." He frowned. "But when I tried to go to a few fights without him, he sent some men after me." He rubbed his ribs, remembering the beating. "The only way out of it is to pay the man off."

"You think he'll stop at that?" She leaned forward and whispered. "From what I've heard about men like that, they won't."

He looked at her and chuckled. "Where have you heard about men like him?"

She leaned back, and he watched her chin go up. "Books. I've read a lot about gangs, and he sounds like your typical gang leader."

He chuckled. "Really?" He reached over and took her hand. "Well, until I have the money to pay Randy off, we won't worry about it."

She frowned. "You'll be careful tomorrow, right?"

He nodded. "I always am."

When their food arrived, he watched her cut into the juicy steak and his mouth watered as he watched her shiny lips nibble on the meat. She had a sexy way about her when she ate, and he couldn't stop watching. By the time they were done with dinner, he was wishing they'd eaten closer to the hotel.

Holly looked at Travis from the corner of her eyes as they entered the lobby of the hotel. When they entered the elevators, he stood in the back as another couple got in behind them. The other couple got out on their floor and as the doors shut, Travis pulled her close and kissed her until she felt her head spin.

"You look amazing tonight," he whispered in her ear. "I couldn't keep my eyes off you."

She moaned and ran her hands through his hair. Then the doors opened, and they stepped apart. He took her hand and walked down the short hallway to their suite.

When he unlocked the door, she moved to set her purse on the table by the door, but he was there. His mouth was hot on hers, and he kissed her until she dropped her purse on the floor, forgotten. Then he backed her up against the wall as his hands ran over her. When she felt her knees shake, he spun her around quickly, so she was facing the wall.

"Put your hands here." He held them up, so she was holding herself a foot from the wall. "Now, don't move," he said next to her ear. His hands roamed over her as he trailed kisses down the column of her neck, between her shoulder blades, and down to her thighs. He slowly pulled her skirt up until she felt the cool air on her exposed skin.

His fingers snaked her silk panties aside as they reached around to the front of her and dipped into her heat, causing her to rest her forehead on the wall. He used his feet to spread her legs a little wider before he knelt down behind her. When he started running kisses up the backside of her thigh, she felt herself jump in anticipation.

She tried to dig into the wall with her fingers to hold herself steady. Her eyes closed on a moan as his lips trailed across her left cheek and his fingers continued to dip in and out of her. She arched her back as his mouth trailed closer to where she wanted him to kiss her.

"Yes, open for me," he groaned just before his tongue darted out and licked a trail across her upper thigh until it finally reached where his fingers were. She bent at the waist further, exposing more of her for his tongue.

"You taste so good. Just like honey," he said, trailing his mouth over every inch of her.

"Travis, please." She felt his hands run up and down her legs as he used his mouth on her.

Then his mouth was gone, and she instantly wished for it back. She heard him stand behind her and unzip his pants, and then he was inside her and nothing else mattered. He pushed her up against the wall, holding her tight around the waist as he reached around and used his fingertips on the tight nub of her sex until she felt herself explode around him.

"More," he growled and spread her legs wider. She was on her toes and desperately holding onto his arms since her legs had turned to jelly after her orgasm. With each thrust, he went deeper, stronger, as he pumped his hips against her over and over. She tried to hold off for him, but it was all just too much for her.

When she recovered this time, she realized he was still behind her. She couldn't hear or see yet since all of her senses had fled her, but she knew he'd followed her the last time.

"If we don't move, we'll end up sleeping on the floor." He chuckled.

"You move first." She opened her eyes and was happy to see the wall. "Good, I haven't lost my sight or hearing."

He chuckled again. "No, but I think I broke a few rules of etiquette."

"Hmm?" She turned around and wrapped her arms around him as they leaned against the wall.

"I'm usually smoother than this." He nodded to where they were, and she laughed.

"I'm not complaining."

"No." He looked down into her eyes. "No, you're not."

CHAPTER 9

The next morning, Holly woke up to an empty bed. There was a note on Travis' pillow. She rolled over and read it.

Sorry for taking off early, but I've got to hit the gym one last time. I should be back around noon, and then I have to head out for the night. If you're around, maybe we can do lunch here. Go spend some of that money you've won.

Enjoy... Travis

She smiled and looked up at the ceiling. Maybe she would go spend her money. After all, she'd never been in a large city like this before. There were bound to be places she could go and entertain herself for the next few hours.

Jumping from the bed, she showered and dressed quickly. She hit the little stores along her block first and by the time she made it back up to the room at eleven thirty, both of her arms were full of bags. She'd even bought a few things for Travis. She'd never seen so many stores in her life; it was so hard to stop herself from spending more than the three hundred dollars she'd limited herself to. She'd never spent that much in her life but figured since she'd won it, it couldn't hurt.

When she walked into the room, Travis was already there with a table of food set out on the balcony.

"Hi." He chuckled. "Wow." He rushed over and helped her with her bags. "Do you think you got enough?"

She laughed. "I'm a woman, we never have enough."

"I ordered us lunch. I've got to be across town in an hour."

She frowned. "Does the fight start that soon?"

He shook his head. "I've got a meeting with Randy, and we have to go over a few things before."

"Oh." She set the last of her bags down and instantly felt depressed. She'd really hoped that he'd let her go.

"Come on." He took her hand and she followed him out to the balcony.

They sat out on the balcony in the sun and she ate her chicken salad, wishing more than anything that he'd change his mind.

"I'm not going to change my mind." He looked over at her and when she looked at him questioningly, he said, "It's written all over your face." He chuckled a little.

"It's just a fight. I've seen plenty on TV."

He shook his head and looked down at his empty plate. "You'll distract me."

"Oh, I never thought of it like that." Knowing she could distract him made her smile a little.

"I'll be back late, but we will still have most of the day tomorrow to do something else. Maybe we'll go see a show?"

She nodded. "That would be fun."

"Promise me you'll stay close to the hotel. There are parts of the city that you wouldn't want to find yourself in after dark."

She nodded. "I think I'll try my hand at the tables. I've been watching the gambling shows and have always wanted to try blackjack.

He shook his head. "I could never win a dime on those tables. You'll probably win the house." He chuckled then stood. "I have to go." He walked over and leaned down to kiss her. He held her still and looked into her eyes for a moment, and she saw the fear and anxiety in his dark eyes. "I'll be back. One more for luck." He kissed her and this time she felt everything he was feeling. She sat there and listened to the hotel door shut and still didn't move. Her knees had gone weak and her mind refused to stop thinking about the kiss.

Did he know that she loved him? How had she fallen so quickly? Especially for him?

She leaned her head down on the glass table. She felt like crying. She was doomed. She just knew there was no way he was feeling the same way about her. Sure, he was nervous and anxious about the fight, but after the renovations on her store and the theater were finished, he was more than likely hitting the road again. She wasn't.

She'd told him the truth. She belonged in Fairplay. There had been a time when she wanted nothing more than to get out of the small town. Actually, up until earlier that year, she'd been trying to think of ways to sell the shop and head down to Florida or take a tour of Europe. She'd heard her friends talking about wanting to do that, so she'd started reading books on it and had dreamed of it ever since.

Now, however, she wanted nothing more than to settle down in Fairplay in her apartment above her bookstore and spend as much time with Travis as she could.

When she finally got up and stepped inside, she had decided that she needed to treat herself tonight. She walked up the stairs and showered and dressed in the sexy red dress she'd brought to wear to the fight, just in case Travis had changed his mind. She piled her red hair up in a curly mass and let several wisps spring loose.

When she stepped out of the elevator two hours later, she felt confident. She noticed a few men turn their heads and watch her walk towards the blackjack tables. When she sat down, she was immediately engulfed in the world of the game. Her worry about Travis disappeared.

Four hours later there was a small crowd gathered around the table. People cheered as she flipped her cards over and won yet another hand. She was almost ten thousand dollars up from her initial two hundred dollars.

She sipped her cherry coke and nibbled on the French fries she'd ordered. Still, her mind was so focused on the table she didn't register that someone new had come up behind her until he placed a hand on her shoulder.

"Miss Bridles?"

She looked around to see a very large Mexican man standing over her. "Yes?" Her first thought was that she'd done something wrong during the game.

"I'm here on behalf of Travis."

"Oh?" Worry instantly shot through her. "Is everything alright?"

"Yes," he nodded. "If you'll be so kind as to cash out and come with me."

She looked at him. "You haven't told me your name." She waved the dealer away from dealing her another hand.

"I'm Randy, Travis' agent, and manager."

"Did he get hurt?" She stood and started to gather her chips.

"Miss," the dealer broke in, "if you want, we can cash these out for you and credit them to your room. You can get the funds when you check out." The dealer looked towards Randy with a nod.

"Yes, please. Thank you," she said and signed the receipt for her chips. Then she turned back to Randy. "Is he hurt?"

"No, ma'am. The fight starts in an hour. If you'll join me, I'll take you to him."

She frowned. "But he doesn't want me there."

"He's had a change of heart," he said, taking her arm rather firmly in his big hands.

"If you'll just wait, I can call…" She started to pull her cell phone out of her handbag.

"I don't think you fully understand what I'm saying." He jerked her arm. She cried out a little and felt something jab in her side. "Come with me now."

She nodded and thought of a million ways she'd been taught to get away from a situation like this. None of them involved having your boyfriend in trouble. No matter what she did, they still had Travis and she wouldn't rest until she knew that he was safe.

"I don't understand. He's here. He's going to fight. Why do you need me?"

"Insurance." He jerked her arm until they stepped outside onto the sidewalk. They walked around the side of the hotel and stopped in front of a dark sedan. He opened the back door and motioned for her to get in. "It would be beneficial if you cooperate."

She glared at him and got in. When he got in next to her, she spoke up. "If this is about the fifteen thousand, I can pay you."

He laughed. "I don't need your money or his. I make more than triple that for one fight. Especially if it involves Travis. He's a star you know." The man looked over at her.

"Then you have no intention of letting him go?" She bit her bottom lip.

"No, not until he's no longer useful to me. And he's been on a winning streak. He's a sure win tonight."

She glared at him and tried to think as the car drove them quickly out of town. She tried to remember landmarks, but it was too dark, and everything was going by too fast.

By the time they pulled off the road, she was completely and helplessly lost. When they stepped out of the car, the heat of the dessert hit her, and her heels sank in the soft sand. There were over a hundred cars parked around a small building that looked like an old car wash.

"Come with me." Randy grabbed her arm again. She jerked it away.

"There's no need to be rude." She glared up at him and he dropped his arm and nodded.

"Fine. This way." He motioned for her to follow him. They walked around the building and entered the back door.

The room was brightly lit. They walked down a long hallway and when Randy opened a door, she saw Travis sitting on a bench, having his hands taped.

When he saw her, he frowned and stood. "What's this about?"

"We thought it would be helpful if your lady friend joined us tonight."

"I don't want her here." He sat back down and nodded to have the man finish taping up his fists. She was shocked at Travis' attitude. He'd dismissed her like it was the most natural thing for her to be kidnapped and dragged into the desert.

"She stays," Randy said, pushing her a step further into the room. She almost fell when her heel snagged on the floor. Travis was up quickly, gathering her in his arms.

"Sorry about this," he whispered to her.

She nodded and held onto him. He made sure she was steady on her feet and then moved closer to Randy.

"Regardless of what happens tonight, this is the last time I'll fight for you." He stood his ground.

"You're finished when I say you are. Besides, there's a little matter of the money you owe me."

"I offered you the money on the ride over here." She stepped forward, only to be pushed behind Travis. "He doesn't want the money," she said to his back.

Travis looked at Randy. "I mean it. This is the last time." Randy laughed and waved him away. "Holly sits where I can see her and we leave together."

Randy looked at her. "Such a pretty little thing. Much prettier than the blonde you brought along last time."

Holly's stomach dropped with the knowledge that Travis had brought Savannah to a fight. Why hadn't he wanted her to come along? She kept her eyes focused on Travis' back as the men argued. When Travis turned back around and pulled her next to him as he sat to have his other hand taped, she could feel him vibrating with anger.

When they walked from the room, he pulled her close and whispered. "No matter what happens, stay put in your chair. Don't move from it. I mean it, Holly. Not until I come and get you."

She nodded as they walked into a large room filled with people cheering. The cage was bigger than she'd imagined it would be. They looked so much smaller on TV. He walked her over to a corner chair and sat her down.

"Stay here." He leaned down and before he kissed her quickly, he said, "I'm sorry you were dragged into this."

She watched him step into the cage and the crowd went wild, chanting his name over and over.

She sat there in her fancy red dress with her sexy black heels and wished to be anywhere but there. She closed her eyes and felt her stomach turn. Why had she wanted to come along tonight?

When the cheering died down, she opened her eyes and finally saw Travis' opponent. He was built a lot like Travis but had bigger muscles and a long scar running down the left side of his face. She felt herself shiver in the overly hot room. Wrapping her arms around herself, she watched the events unfold, holding her breath. She just knew that Travis wouldn't win this fight. Not when so much was on the line.

When the fighting began, she couldn't even blink. The two men circled around until Travis threw the first punch, then the other man was on him and they were falling to the mat. She stood up and gasped as everyone around her stood to cheer. Her hands covered her mouth so she couldn't scream as she watched Travis roll around on the floor, trying to get the upper hand with the larger man.

Just when it looked like he'd finally gotten the man into a hold, he would outmaneuver him and Travis would have to fling himself around again and start all over. He managed to get in a few punches just before the man used his elbow to knock Travis loose. When Travis fell backward, the other man was on him, holding him down and hitting him over and over again in the face.

She closed her eyes and looked away, trying to focus on anything other than what was happening a few feet from her. She heard bones crunch, heard blood splatter as fists hit skin. When she turned back around, she was shocked to see Travis on top of the other man, jabbing him over and over. The man's face was turning red as Travis held him in a chokehold, twisting around so he wouldn't get knocked off again.

Just when she thought it would end, the man wiggled free, rolled over, and stood up. Travis jumped to his feet and dodged the first blow, which was aimed at his head, barely dodging the second one and taking a third blow in the gut.

Bending down, he hugged the man until they fell back to the mat together with Travis on top. All the TV fights couldn't have prepared her for what she was seeing, what she was feeling as she watched Travis receive and deliver blow after blow.

Finally, Travis was able to move around again and get the larger man in a chokehold again. When the other man's face started turning red, he tapped Travis on the head and Travis backed off.

Blood dripped from the side of Travis' left eye, and his

eye looked swollen as the referee held up his arm, signaling his win.

Instantly, Travis' eyes locked on hers. She felt her knees go weak as she sank back down into her chair. She sat there as the crowd cheered for him and then quieted back down, and then they all stood and started cheering the next fight. Still, she sat there and waited for Travis.

When he finally came for her, he had changed into his street clothes. He had a small white bandaged over the cut on his left eye.

"Let's go," he said, pulling her towards the door. When they stepped outside, Randy and two other large men were standing there waiting for them. Sheer terror ran through her body.

"Let it go, Randy," Travis said, pushing her behind him.

"You know I can't do that. Not after the haul you just proved you could bring in."

"I'm done," Travis said, taking a step closer. "You're done. This is all over."

"It's over when I say it is," Randy yelled. "I made you. You owe me." The man took a step towards him and pulled a gun out of his jacket. "We'll just go for a long ride in the dessert." He looked over at Holly and she knew what he was threatening. "Then maybe you'll change your mind."

Just then there was a flood of lights, blinding them all. The whole dirt parking lot was filled as people shouted. Travis pushed her back inside the door just as the first shot sounded. His body covered hers as they fell to the ground. People ran past them, screaming, as Travis rolled them and finally stood up and pushed her against the corner, shielding her from the crowd.

"Should we be running?" she yelled over the loud noise.

"No, not this time." He looked down at her. "I'm really sorry about this."

She reached up and took his face in her hands. "It's okay. I won enough money tonight to bail us out." She smiled.

He laughed and shook his head. "We won't need it."

"Oh?" She watched as a flood of police officers stormed into the dark room.

"Nope." He turned and grabbed her hand. Then they walked towards the officers who were cuffing a group of college-aged kids. "Where's Martin?" he asked one of them who looked at him and then nodded towards the front door. "Outside." The man went back to cuffing the men.

"Travis?" She looked up at him.

"It's okay. He's the cop that saved my life, remember?"

She nodded. "But, I don't…"

He shook his head. "I'll explain later."

CHAPTER 10

*M*uch later they sat in the back of a police car as they traveled back down the highway towards their hotel. She still had questions after long hours of giving their statements to Detective Martin.

Finally, they were released and sent back to their hotel room. When they walked into the lobby, he took her hand in his and they rode the elevator in silence.

When they stepped into the room, he pulled her close and hugged her. "I know you have a lot of questions, but I think we both deserve a long hot shower first."

She pulled back and looked down at her ruined red dress and nodded.

"What a shame." He looked at her dress. "I think this was my favorite." He took her hand as she slipped out of her heels and followed him up the stairs. She noticed that the sun was just coming up.

"So much for spending the day seeing a show," he said, nodding to the sunrise. "We'll be lucky if we get enough sleep before our flight tonight."

Her head ached and when he peeled her dress from her, she leaned her head down on his shoulder and closed her eyes.

When they stepped into the warm spray, he groaned and held his head under the water. She noticed a few bruises had already popped up over his ribs, not to mention that his left eye was almost completely swollen shut now.

He pulled her close and held still under the warm spray. "I'm sorry about tonight."

She shook her head. "I think I get it. Why you didn't want me to come tonight." She pulled back and looked up at him.

"Oh?" He pushed her wet hair from her face.

She nodded. "You knew the police were going to raid the place."

He laughed. "You could say that. I told them where it was when it was. They'd known about the fights for a while but could never catch up to them. I just wish they'd had better timing and had gotten there before I went into the cage." He touched his eye then shook his head and dumped some shampoo over their heads and began to scrub. "I called Martin last week after you suggested it. I walked into the police station this morning after I ditched the men Randy had trailing me. I'm sorry they saw us together." He shook his head. "Now they'll have him for attempted murder." He stopped and pulled her closer. "God!"

She rested her head on his shoulder and enjoyed the feeling of him holding her. Then he pulled back and said, "You must be exhausted." She nodded, looking into his dark eyes.

"Let's get you dried off." He helped rinse the soap

from her hair, then flipped off the shower and grabbed the towel.

She stood there motionless as he dried her off and walked her into the bedroom. "So," she started to say as he handed her one of his shirts to put on to sleep in, "you won't be going to jail?"

He stopped and looked at her. "No. I'll have to come back and testify, but no." He shook his head. "I'm free to go home tomorrow."

She liked the sound of that. Home. She crawled into bed next to him and snuggled down and fell asleep listening to his heartbeat.

When she woke, she was alone. She frowned at the pillow, expecting a note, but there wasn't one. Rolling out of bed, she went to the restroom and dressed quickly. When she looked at the time, she realized she had less than an hour before they needed to leave for the airport.

When she walked out into the living room, her bags tucked under her arms, she was shocked to see Travis sitting at a table that was fully stocked with wonderful smelling food.

"I thought we'd have one last meal here." He stood up and walked over to take her bags.

"It looks and smells wonderful." She sat down at the table overlooking the busy street below them.

"I thought..." She shook her head, realizing she'd been a fool. Of course, he wouldn't have left her in Vegas.

He tilted his head and looked at her. She knew she had to say something. "I thought we wouldn't have time to eat. This is a wonderful surprise."

She looked down at the blueberry pancakes and smiled. "Mmm, my favorite," she said, digging in. "I had forgotten that I went without dinner last night. I had planned on treating myself to a big meal." She bit into the sweetness and sighed.

"I'm sorry we didn't get to see a show." He frowned down at his food.

"Well, it kind of was a show last night." He looked up as she reached over and took his hand. "How does the eye feel?" She nodded to his face.

He reached up and touched it and, then smiled. "Not bad. He hit like a girl. At least it doesn't hurt as bad as when you punched me." She laughed.

The flight back to Texas seemed quicker than the flight to Vegas had. She didn't think she was still tired, after having slept most of the day away, but when Travis woke her before they landed, she realized she was still exhausted.

"I never realized that being kidnapped and being in a raid could be so tiring." She smiled and helped him carry her bags to his car.

"Yeah, it takes a lot of out a person."

"I think I could sleep the rest of the day away. Well, maybe after a quick stop at Mama's for some fried food."

He laughed. "You know, that does sound good."

"Oh, right. You're a free man now. No more training." She clapped her hands. "Oh! I almost forgot. I'm a rich woman now."

"Oh?" He looked over at her.

She nodded. "I won big last night before Randy and his goons came along."

He turned out of the airport parking lot and smiled over at her. "How much did you win?"

"Ten thousand dollars."

He gasped and looked over at her. "You? You won ten thousand?"

"Yup." She smiled. "Who would have thought that I'd be good at blackjack?"

He laughed and shook his head. "Man remind me to take you to Atlantic City next time I go."

"I'd love to. You know, I think I could possibly make a career out of it."

"What? Gambling?"

"Hmm…" She thought about it. "Well, maybe not. I'm not sure I could stand it if I lost." He smiled.

"I'm glad you went along with me."

"Oh?"

"You made something good come out of something not so good. If you hadn't come along, I wouldn't have had the guts to go into Martin's office and set up the sting. Do you know that he remembered me?" He shook his head. "He told me that I had turned out pretty well."

"Of course, you have." She leaned back in the seat and looked at him.

He glanced over at her. "He talked to you a lot. I think he liked you."

She smiled. "He couldn't stop talking about how much you reminded him of his son. I guess he lost him overseas in the Gulf war. He even felt somewhat responsible about you getting caught up in the whole cage fighting mess."

"Really? He had nothing to do with it."

"Yeah, he said after they'd let you go he'd meant to check in on you, but he'd gotten caught up in a case."

"You know it's strange how a stranger can affect your life so much."

She nodded and let out a large yawn. "I'm sorry. "I haven't been this tired in a long time."

"I know what you mean. Just another hour and we'll be home."

"That sounds good." She looked out of the window and all she could see now were pine trees zipping by her.

"Why didn't you go away to college?" she asked, trying to keep her mind alert.

"I was too busy partying with my friends."

"I always wanted to go to college. I think I would have enjoyed it."

"What did you want to study?" he asked, glancing at her.

She smiled over at him. "Business, I suppose. You?"

"Architecture. Like my dad. I guess it's in the blood. I did take a year of online classes before I left town. But when my grades started slipping due to my drinking…" He shrugged his shoulders. "I wouldn't mind going back. I've enjoyed working the last few weeks on your place and the theater."

"Do you think you'll stay in town, now that you don't have to pay Randy off?"

He looked over at her. "No. I don't belong there anymore. I'll finish my dad's projects, sell everything, and move on."

She felt her heart drop a little. "Where will you go?"

He shrugged his shoulders again. "Not sure, yet. I guess I have some time to think about it, though."

"Yeah," She looked out the window and tried to hide her disappointment.

❆

By the time they drove into town, Travis' eyes were burning, and he wished more than anything that he'd gotten a good night's sleep. But instead of drifting off like Holly had, he'd lain awake, staring at the ceiling and replaying everything that they'd been through that evening. It had been too close.

One thing he'd promised himself since leaving Fairplay four years ago was that no one would ever get harmed because of him again.

Last night had made him realize that he was no better than his mother. Sure, she had flipped her lid mentally, but he'd allowed himself to be sucked into a dangerous world and then he'd taken Holly into that world, and she could have been killed.

He knew he had a few more months in town, but he had to make sure he didn't do anything stupid again to put her in danger.

When they pulled into Mama's, his stomach growled loudly, causing Holly to laugh. "I know how you feel. Those pancakes have already worn off and I'm starved."

"Maybe it'll be meatloaf night. I haven't had good meatloaf since I left town." He raced around and opened her door.

"Willard does make the best in Texas," she said, talking about the cook at Mama's. The man had a knack for making barbeque meatloaf. No one in town knew his secrets. There was a rumor that not even Jamella, aka Mama, knew what he put in there to make it so good.

They sat at one of the only empty booths near the back. "I guess you are a lucky charm," he said, nodding to the menu board. "Meatloaf night." Half the town was in

Mama's, filling themselves with barbeque meatloaf and Jamella's homemade apple pie.

Holly waved at Alex and Grant, who were sitting across the room with their daughter. He didn't know the little girl's name, but she was the spitting image of her mother.

"They're having another," she said, smiling over at the family. He frowned and looked over at the couple.

"Another kid?"

She nodded. "I know you guys were engaged, but I just wanted you to know that she found a good man." She nodded to Grant. "Some things are just meant to be, you know?" She leaned her chin on her hands. "Just like you were meant to go to Vegas and get cleaned up."

He thought about it and for the first time, he could see the pattern. He knew that he'd been no good for Alex. Hell, he'd cheated on her more times than even he could remember. But in his mind, he had loved her. Loved being in love. Maybe that's why he had avoided being with another woman for so long. He looked across the table at Holly and realized he'd fallen into the trap again. Not that he was in love with her. At least he didn't think he was…yet. But he had strong feelings for her already. Like he'd had for Alex and even Savannah in a twisted way.

He took a sip of his iced tea and tried to think about something else. But as Holly looked across the table at him, he kept telling himself that he was getting in too deep.

Just as they were finishing up their dinner, Billy and Corey walked in with two girls on their arms. His old friends were dressed in their nice Levi's and button up shirts. He didn't recognize the girls but guessed that they were probably a few years younger than they were.

"Hey, Travis," Corey called out and moved towards them. "Wow, man. Who gave you that shiner?"

He'd forgotten about his eye and reached up to touch it. "Happened in Vegas," he said, absentmindedly.

"Wow, did you just get back from Vegas?" Billy asked and then looked at Holly. "The two of you?" Billy waved his eyebrows in a way that only Billy could. Travis wished he could reach up and yank the furry things from his face.

"Yeah, business trip," he said and tried to dismiss the group. "Shall we get going?" he asked Holly, who nodded and stood up.

"Oh, man. Don't run off on our account. We were just going to grab some grub and take the girls up to the cabin. Maybe you guys would like to join us?"

"Not tonight." He stood and took Holly's hand in his. "Night." He nodded to his old friends and went to pay for dinner.

"I understand you don't want to hang out with your old friends, but you could have been a little nicer about it," she said when they were in the car.

"What?" He glanced at her as he drove the block and a half to the house.

"Travis, you were rude to them." She crossed her arms over her chest and looked at him.

"They're used to it," he said, parking in front of the garage. "I'm heading in to get some sleep." He nodded to the big house and then walked around and grabbed their bags from the trunk.

"That's fine with me." She grabbed her bag from him. "I understand you being rude to them, but there's no reason to be rude to me." She started walking away. He dropped his bag and spun her around.

"I'm not being rude to you." He shook his head. "Can't you see I'm like those guys?" He ran his hand through his hair, thinking about pulling it out. "I'm trouble. I'll probably cheat on you. I might even fall back to my old smoking, drinking ways." He took a few steps away and threw his arms up. "Go." He waved his arms away. "Go get some sleep." He grabbed his bag and rushed into the house.

When he shut the door behind him, he felt like punching something. The door pushed against his shoulders hard. He stepped aside and threw it open to see a very mad Holly standing there.

"How dare you walk away without giving me a chance to talk." She put her hands on her hips and glared at him. Then she stepped into the house and pointed her finger into his chest. "You think you're the only one who has issues." She took another step towards him when he backed up. "You think you're so bad?" She used both hands to shove him back another step. "I'll tell you something, Travis Nolan. I've dealt with you before. You may not remember every time you were an ass to me, but I do and I can assure you that you're not the same person." She shoved him again until he fell back and landed on the sofa sideways, his legs hanging over the arm. She moved around until she stood over him. "You may think that you'll have a lapse, but I know you better than you know yourself. You've spent the last four years cleaning your body of all the poisons you shoved into it because of those two baboons. You are not like them and will never be again." She turned to leave. "And if you think this is over, guess again."

He stopped her before she reached the door and spun

her around. When she opened her mouth to yell some more, he covered it with his own. He put everything he'd been feeling since seeing her standing in the doorway of the old car wash in the sexy red number behind the kiss. He pushed her up against the doorway, almost knocking down several of his mother's paintings on the wall. When he yanked her jacket off her shoulders, she gasped. He heard something rip as he pulled her clothing from her quickly.

Finally, what seemed like hours later, she stood before him naked, and he pulled her up and walked back towards the couch. When they fell onto the soft cushion, she moaned and pulled his jeans from his hips.

"Now," she groaned. "Now, Travis." She looked up into his eyes and he realized he would have given anything to her at that moment. Anything.

CHAPTER 11

"Tell me everything that happened in Vegas," Missy said with a look of anticipation on her face. Holly had needed a little time to herself but having dinner with her best friend and her fiancé was second best, at eating a whole cheesecake alone.

She laughed. "Where to begin?" She leaned back on the deck chair and started to tell her friend everything that had happened as she looked off to their backyard. Reece had bought the old place earlier that year and they were still doing major repairs to the place. But, like the bookstore, it was coming along quickly.

"Oh my god!" Missy looked at her with her eyes wide. "Are you okay?"

Holly laughed. "I'm fine, really."

"I can't believe it." She shook her head. "I've never met anyone who's lived through something like that. It's almost straight out of a movie."

"Yeah, I guess so." She giggled. "Underground in Vegas," she said in her best broadcasting voice.

Melissa chuckled. "Well, I can't believe it. You actually look great." She leaned back and took another sip. "If something like that had happened to me, I'd be a wreck."

"Oh, please. You're Miss Cool under pressure. I've seen you work at the clinic, remember?"

Missy smiled. "Being a nurse doesn't mean you know how to keep your cool when there are people kidnapping you or shooting at you."

"They weren't actually shooting at us." She shook her head. "Anyway, your place is coming along great." She waved her glass to the back of the house.

"Yeah, Reece is in there hammering away on the bathroom. He wants the new bathtub installed before we get married." Melissa set her glass down and then squealed. "It still gets me." She shook her head. "Sorry."

Holly laughed. "That's okay. Have you found out anything about Ryan yet?"

Melissa shook her head no. "We heard from the private investigator's daughter that they were working on it, but other than that, nothing more."

She leaned back. "I'm sure you'll find Ryan before your wedding."

"I just hope he's okay." She leaned forward and whispered. "The last time I saw him he had two bullet holes in his stomach."

"Maybe it was a misunderstanding. I mean, look at everything I went through in Vegas. Maybe Ryan really isn't in trouble with the law."

Missy leaned back and took another drink. "I hope so. It's just weird that the police signed him out like he was in custody." She shook her head. "Reece would be heartbroken to know that his brother was on the wrong side of the law."

She thought about Travis and knew that if he was still his old self, she wouldn't be with him. "Let me know when you find something out."

She thought about their conversation on her short drive home. So much was still undetermined in her relationship with Travis. She didn't know how much longer she could stand not knowing where they were headed. Was he going to leave town like he was talking about, or was there was a possibility of him sticking around?

She parked her car in front of the garage and flipped off her lights. Frowning, she got out and looked at the empty spot where his car usually sat. Maybe he took his friends up on their offer? She grabbed her bag from the seat and locked her car. They needed some time apart; after all, they'd spent the last week together. He was bound to get bored with her sooner or later.

She unlocked her door and flipped on the light. She gasped and took a step backward when she saw the damage. Her sofa was upside down, and her dishes were broken and in a pile on the floor. Her clothes were thrown around the room and covered in something dark and gooey. She closed the door and rested her forehead on it, struggling to fight back the tears. When her hands stopped shaking and her mind finally kicked into gear, she pulled out her cell phone and called the sheriff.

She crawled back in her car and locked the door behind her, as he'd told her to do. A short while later a car pulled in behind her, but it seemed too soon to be the sheriff. Between the headlights and the darkness, she couldn't tell what kind of car it was, and she tensed when she heard the door open. She jumped at the knock on her window and was relieved to see Travis standing there.

"Everything okay?" he asked. When she rolled down her window and he saw her face, he yanked open her door and pulled her out. "What? What's happened?"

"My—" She shook her head. "Someone broke into my apartment."

"What?" He released her and started to head up the stairs.

"Wait." She raced after him. "The sheriff told me to not go in."

He glanced at her and frowned. "He said that to you, not me." He used his key and unlocked the door. "Was it locked when you got here?"

She thought about it. "Yes, I remember unlocking it."

He opened the door and stepped into the lit room. "Damn." He looked around. "I liked that couch." He walked around and then disappeared into the back as she stood in the doorway.

"I told you to stay in your car," the sheriff said behind her, causing her to scream and jump. She covered her mouth and her heart with her hands, and Travis rushed from the back with a baseball bat in his hands.

"Don't scare me like that." She punched the sheriff on the shoulder.

Sheriff Miller frowned. "Sorry." He turned and nodded to Travis. "Evening."

Travis set the bat down. "No one's here."

Travis sat in the big kitchen in his parents' house and tried to be patient with the questions Sheriff Miller asked. When did they leave the house? What time did they return? Did they see anything? He'd answered fewer questions when he'd turned over the underground cage fighting ring.

Holly sat next to him, sipping on a soda and looking tired and scared. She had dealt with being threatened with a gun better than someone breaking in and trashing her stuff.

He couldn't prove it, but he had a sinking feeling that it was his fault. There were a handful of people who came to mind when the sheriff asked if he knew who could have done this.

He mentioned some names and watched Holly's expression.

"You really think Savannah could have done all that?" she asked when he mentioned her name. "She's…" Holly looked towards the sheriff.

"Pregnant?" he said, smiling. "Everyone in town knows."

Travis felt a weird sensation run down his body and without thinking, he blurted out. "It's not mine."

The sheriff looked at him. His gray eyebrows shot up, and then he smiled. "That's good to know. It seems to be the assumption around town. But under the circumstances, it isn't surprising." He wrote something down on his pad of paper and Travis felt his face turn beet red.

For the first time since coming back, he cared what others thought of him. At least where Savannah and her condition were concerned. He didn't want anyone thinking he was irresponsible. Not anymore.

"Now, what's all this about Vegas?" The sheriff looked at him and he groaned. Now it would be several more hours before he ate anything because he'd have to explain everything.

"Do you mind if I make a sandwich?" He stood up and walked to the kitchen when the sheriff nodded. For the next hour they explained everything again and by the time the sheriff finally drove off, Travis had a splitting headache.

"I guess…" Holly started to say, looking towards the back door.

"You can stay here," he said, knowing what she was thinking. "There are two spare rooms. Pick one." He turned and put his plate in the dishwasher, something that was still ingrained in him from his childhood.

She nodded and turned to walk down the hallway but stopped and looked back. "Are you upset with me?"

"Why would I be?"

She shrugged her shoulders and shook her head. "I'm not sure."

"I'm trouble. You're better off steering clear of me until I leave."

"It's not your fault, you know." She took a step towards him.

"What?" He leaned against the countertop and rubbed his forehead.

"Everything. Vegas. My apartment." She nodded towards the garage.

He laughed and turned to get the bottle of aspirin from the cabinet. "Sure, it is. I have jacked up friends. I'm sure they trashed my place to get to me."

"Have you ever thought that maybe it was just a robbery?" She took another step towards him.

He downed a couple of aspirin and shook his head. "Doubtful."

"Does it hurt that bad?" She nodded to his head when he looked confused. He dropped his hand and realized he'd been trying to peel his skin off his forehead.

"I get migraines for a few days following a fight."

"I can help," she said, taking his hand and walking him back towards the couch. He sat down when she pushed him backward. "Relax." She knelt beside him and started rubbing his shoulders.

"What do my back and neck have to do with a migraine?"

"You'd be surprised. I've read several books on the subject. Did you know that this pressure point"—she pushed her thumb into a spot on his back and he felt his head spin—"if pressed hard enough can cause a man to pass out?" He believed it; when she moved her hand, he felt light-headed. "Here, lie down." She pulled his shirt over his head and motioned for him to lay down on his stomach. "Put your arms here." She moved his arms, so they lay next to his body.

Her hands roamed over his sore muscles until every inch of him was relaxed. She talked to him the entire time about pressure points and what each one did. The sound of her voice was so soothing, he found himself drifting off.

When he woke, the sun was blinding him from the living room window, and he realized he'd fallen asleep face down on the couch. One of his mother's throw blankets was thrown on him, and when he stood up, he realized his headache was completely gone. So were some of the aches and pains he'd had since the fight.

Grabbing his shirt, he headed upstairs for a shower.

When he walked into his parents' room, he stopped. Holly was asleep on the bed. Her long red hair was fanned out over his grandmother's quilt. He stepped closer. Her skin was flawless. Her dark eyelashes closed as he stepped closer. He noticed how pink her lips were, and he remembered how sweet they were, how soft and warm.

She was wearing a green tank top and gray shorts that hugged her bottom perfectly. His eyes roamed over every inch of her, remembering how she felt next to him.

He'd meant it last night—he wasn't good for her. She'd be better off if he left town, and she found someone who wanted to settle down in Fairplay and raise a family. He shook his head and stepped back. She was better off with anyone else but him.

He turned away from the sweet sight of her and decided he'd deal with the pink bathroom and shower down the hallway.

CHAPTER 12

It took Holly and Melissa all day to clean her apartment. Half of her clothes were destroyed, including some of the new shoes she'd bought in Vegas that she hadn't even had a chance to wear yet. She controlled her emotions until Missy left, and then she locked her door with the new deadbolt Reece had installed and walked into the bathroom and cried in the shower.

She couldn't wait until her apartment was done, so she could go back home and feel safe again. After dragging herself out of the shower, she put on her thickest pair of sweats and crawled into her new sheets and comforter and watched cartoons until she fell asleep.

The next week, Travis was scarce. He left before sunrise and returned after dark and never stopped by to see her. She seemed to always miss him when he'd stop by the store and check in on the progress. She'd heard he'd been spending a lot of time at the theater but didn't have the heart to stop by and see. She'd noticed he'd moved the

Mustang out into the driveway and on several occasions had heard him pounding away in the house.

Something told her to allow him his space, at least for now. The sheriff stopped by and gave her an update on his search for who had destroyed her stuff. She'd given him a copy of the list of items that she'd given her insurance company.

"If I hadn't sold my old place a few blocks away, last month, I'd have let you stay there," he said, frowning down at her.

She smiled. "That's okay. I'll be fine here. Besides, they'll be done with my apartment next month. They have tripled their efforts there, and I'll be in a whole month before the store is finished."

"That's great news." She followed him out to his car. "Well, if you need anything, just let Jamella or I know." He smiled and waved as he drove away.

She was done for the day and stood in the driveway in the heat. It had been a while since she'd enjoyed the pool and decided to head up and put on her swimsuit. But when she turned to go inside, she heard a car drive up and saw Savannah's Jeep stop in the driveway.

She stood where she was and waited for the other woman to get out of the car.

"How dare you." She slammed the Jeep's door. "How dare you spread lies about me?" Savannah walked over and stopped less than a foot from her.

There was no hiding the fact that she was very pregnant now. The woman's belly stuck out like a beach ball. Her hands and face were swollen and even her ankles were three times the size they used to be. Her long blonde hair was still perfectly in place, as was the layer of caked-on makeup. Her clothes were even tighter now than usual.

"I'm not sure what you're talking about." She stood her ground even though the woman was almost twice her size now.

"You're spreading lies about me. About Travis and I. Telling everyone that he's not the daddy." She rubbed her belly in what was the first maternal action she'd seen.

Holly looked at her and tilted her head. "It's not Travis' baby."

"It is," she almost screamed. "When I visited him in Vegas. Ask him about it." She crossed her arms over her chest. "And you're telling everyone that I broke into your place and trashed it." She nodded to the apartment above the garage.

Holly laughed. "No, I'm not."

Savannah took a step towards her until her face was inches from her own. "You think he'll keep you?" Her eyes raked up and down her. "It's just like before. He'll use you until he's bored and then come running back to me, and we'll be a happy family. Just wait and see. All you are is a warm body to fit his needs."

"Be careful, Savannah," she warned her.

"Or what?" She laughed and leaned back a little. "You've already hit me when I was pregnant. You'll do it again?"

Holly shook her head and stepped back. "No one knew you were pregnant that time."

Savannah laughed and then glared at her. "Tread lightly, little bookworm. No one believes your stories anyway. We all know that Travis is only amusing himself with you. He'll be bored with you soon enough if he already isn't." She turned and got back into her Jeep. It took her a few tries to hoist herself up into the tall vehicle, but finally, she managed it and drove off, peeling out of the driveway.

Holly stood in the driveway, trying not to shake. Everything Savannah said hit too close to home. Travis had been pulling back from her.

Walking up the stairs, she ran over the last conversation they'd had and how he'd warned her that he wasn't good for her. He'd been trying to break it off and she'd been too big of a fool to see it.

All thoughts of a dip in the pool fled, replaced by a strong desire to go riding. Changing into her old jeans and boots, she drove out to Saddleback Ranch, knowing there was always a horse ready to be saddled up at her friends' ranch.

When she drove up, she saw Lauren step off the front porch with a baby in her arms. Emma had just turned one last month and was the spitting image of her mama. Rickie, their son, was running around the yard playing with fire trucks.

"Evening," Lauren said, stepping off the porch.

"Hi." She bent down and picked up Rickie and gave him a sloppy kiss. The boy hugged her back and started chatting about his trucks.

Holly laughed. "Maybe I can play trucks with you later. Right now, I was hoping to go for a ride?" She looked at Lauren.

"Absolutely. You're welcome to take Tanner. He's in the first stall and ready for a run." She nodded towards the barn. "I think you still have a saddle somewhere in there."

She smiled. "Yes, I'll find everything else. Thank

you." She sat Rickie back down and walked towards the barn.

It had been almost six months since she'd ridden—too long. She saddled up Tanner, Lauren's gentle gelding. The horse snuggled with her shoulder as she strapped on the saddle.

She jumped on his back and they bolted from the yard. Holly's mind cleared.

She'd never really thanked Haley for teaching her how to ride, or the West sisters for always having an open door and a horse to take out. Some things just didn't need to be said. The sisters had always been there for her and their friends.

Holly could remember wishing she had two sisters and dreaming that they would be as close as Lauren, Alex, and Haley were. But her mother had always told her that being raised an only child had perks, like more Christmas presents. Holly would have gladly shared her presents if it meant having just one sibling.

Travis was also an only child. He'd been spoiled by his parents, and everyone in town had seen it firsthand. His father had constantly bailed him out of his problems, and his mother had spoiled him all throughout school. She'd attended every school function, and her voice was loud enough to make sure that her son was the star of every play or sporting event.

The woman had always claimed it was her duty as the mayor's wife, but everyone had known it was her devotion to her son that caused her to push so hard. She supposed that, in the end, it had been that devotion that had caused her to go off the deep end and almost kill Grant Holton shortly after he and Alex had started dating, even though it was because Travis had cheated on Alex with Savannah that Alex and Grant had started seeing one another.

Holly slowed the horse down to open a gate so she could ride in the back fields towards the small pond.

Thinking of Travis only caused the hurt to surface again. She'd known what he was, who he was before she'd let her heart get involved. Her mind had screamed at her, warning her to steer clear, but her body had taken over.

She smiled as she closed the gate and kicked the horse into a trot, thinking about Travis' body. He did have one of those heart-stopping, sexy bodies. She'd never been with someone so damn sexy before. Nor had she ever been with someone she'd felt so connected with. The possibility that he didn't feel that connection with her stung.

She leaned down and enjoyed the wind in her face as they rushed towards the other side of the field.

Travis was sore and sweaty again. His arms and back hurt from moving furniture around. He'd cleared out most of the old stuff in the guest rooms and had carried it all down to the garage. He'd had to pull his mother's Mustang out to make room for everything. He thought about having a garage sale to get rid of all the old furniture, but it would have to wait until all the repairs were done inside.

He'd done everything he could over the last week to keep his mind off of Holly. He'd spent most of his time running between the theater and her store. The park had been completed and there was an official grand opening scheduled for a few weeks. He doubted he would attend the event. In his off-hours, he'd locked himself in the house and worked away.

It had taken him a whole day to rip out the old pink tile from the second bathroom. He'd watched video after video on how to repair and tile a tub before he felt confident enough to try it.

He'd made a trip to the Tyler hardware store and gotten everything he needed. When he'd tried to get it all in his little car, he'd wished for his old truck back. He'd ended up putting most of the supplies in the front seat next to him. The hardware planks for the flooring lay across his back seat and the tiles filled up his trunk. He'd hoped the little car would make it back to Fairplay and not conk out on him.

Unloading everything from his car was exhausting since he had to lug it up the spiral staircase and down the long hallway. He'd once loved the layout of the plantation style house with its large rooms, beautiful staircase, and tall ceilings. Now, however, he looked at it all as a lot of work. He had to pull the tall ladder from the garage, so he could repaint the tall ceilings. He had to pay extra to have the large bedrooms re-carpeted. The railing on the staircase had to be sanded and restrained.

He'd convinced Roger to send the drywall guys over to patch up the walls in the bathroom, so he could tile. He'd bought them some beer and had persuaded them to go around the house and patch any other holes they found.

He heated up frozen dinners and fell asleep watching the news in the living room, so he wouldn't think about Holly just a few feet away in the apartment. He'd watched her from the windows a few times, coming and going. Every time he saw her, his desire grew more and more. But he'd gone years keeping himself in line and knew it was just a matter of redirecting his energy. So he busted his butt on the house and went to bed completely exhausted each night.

He knew he couldn't avoid her much longer; after all, she was living at his place. He'd heard from Roger that her place would be move-in ready in less than a month, at which time he planned to put the house on the market. He knew he couldn't leave town until the theater was done, which Roger informed him wouldn't be until next spring.

But he figured he could move back into his apartment after Holly moved out, so he could start showing the house. He didn't think there was much that needed to be done to the apartment since his folks had just built it for him shortly after he'd graduated high school.

He stopped working on hanging the tile and closed his eyes. What a different life he'd had back then. Not only had he gotten anything he'd asked for, but he'd done anything and everything he'd wanted. Living unrestrained had been his biggest desire. That's why he'd moved out in the first place.

The one rule his folks had set for him of not smoking in their house had been enough to cause him to pack up and sleep above the garage. Finally, after he'd lived in the empty space for almost a year, his mother had convinced his father to spend a small fortune to turn it into an apartment for him.

How had he not seen that he was heading down a doomed path? Not only had he been drinking too much, but he'd been smoking more and more. He found an old picture book while cleaning out his mother's sewing room. He'd looked at the images of what he used to be and almost cried. He'd had a growing beer belly and in every picture, he had a cigarette or a beer in his hands. Dependency. He never wanted to feel that dependent on anything ever again.

It took him almost three hours to finish tiling the tub and shower area. When he stood back, he couldn't help but smile. It was perfect. The new dark stone tile would accent the antique white walls he was planning and the new sink and toilet that he planned on installing tomorrow.

When he heard a noise behind him, he jumped and spun around.

"Sorry." Holly stood in the doorway. "I saw that the back door was open, and I was worried."

He frowned. "I guess I didn't shut it after carrying all this in." He nodded to the tile.

"It looks wonderful." She stepped into the room. She looked good in tight faded jeans, an old blue shirt, and riding boots.

"Thanks," he said, trying to get his heart to level off. "Have you been riding?" he asked, nodding to her boots.

"Yes, I was just out at Saddleback. Lauren let me take Tanner out." She sighed. "There's nothing like a long ride to clear your head." She stepped closer to the shower. "How did you do this?" She ran her fingers over the tile.

"Actually, it was pretty easy. I thought I was going to have a hard time with it, but after watching a few videos…" He shrugged his shoulders and realized how sore they were again. His mind flashed to the night she'd given him a back rub and instantly wished for another one.

"Well, you've done a lot on the place so far." She turned and looked at him. "I looked around." She blushed a little. "You know, making sure that nothing was disturbed."

He nodded. "I still have a lot to do."

"If you need any help…" She waited. He didn't know what to say so he just looked at her. "I saw some paint buckets downstairs."

"Yeah." He looked down at his hands and realized they were covered with grout. He dumped them in the bucket of water and scrubbed them clean. "I won't start painting for a few days yet."

"I can help. Until the store is ready I have nothing to do except check in there occasionally."

He shook his head. "I wouldn't want to bother you."

She looked down at her hands. "Actually, I'd enjoy it. I've been going kind of crazy with nothing to do."

"If you want to help, I'll show you what needs to be painted." He dried his hands on a towel and walked down the hallway.

"I bought the big ladder in." He nodded to the beast sitting near the stairs. "I want to get rid of the mint green my mother made my dad paint everywhere. Why anyone would paint their walls pink and green is beyond me. I don't remember the wall colors being a problem when I was a kid, but after moving out on my own, I couldn't stand being in the house with the walls screaming at me." He chuckled.

"My mother painted her kitchen bright yellow and orange." She cringed as he laughed.

"I've got enough paint here." He showed her the four five-gallon buckets. "There are brushes, rollers, and tarps to cover the floors. I've got a few more days' work in the bathroom upstairs." He glanced up the stairs and thought about everything that still needed to be done. "The appraiser was going to stop by later this month.

"So, you're still going to sell the place?" She glanced at him.

"Yeah." He avoided her eyes. "Once the theater is done, I'll be heading out."

She nodded and after a moment she said, "I'll start first thing in the morning."

He nodded, not sure what else to say. She started walking out, but he stopped her. "Have you had dinner?"

She glanced over her shoulder. "Yes, I ate with Lauren and her family."

He nodded and watched her leave, knowing it was for the best. He didn't know what had caused him to blurt it out, but something had demanded that he stop her from leaving. His body reacted every time he saw her, and he cursed it for its weakness. He knew he needed to control it, and so far, the only that had been successful in helping him do so was physical labor. So he started hauling the large boxes of flooring up the stairs, determined to sweat his desire for Holly out so he could get some sleep that night.

CHAPTER 13

*H*olly didn't want Travis to know that she was totally excited about painting. In a few weeks she'd be painting her place and be completely overwhelmed by it, but for now, she wanted nothing more than to cover inch by inch of the mint green walls with the soft white.

She'd knocked on the back door just before sunrise, her hair tied up in a purple handkerchief. Her faded jeans and white paint shirt were soft and comfortable along with her old sneakers. She had even brought a soda and snacks for later since she doubted she'd want to stop working for a while.

When Travis opened the back door, her smile faltered a little. "Are you okay?" She stepped in, worried.

"Yeah," he stepped back. "Why?"

She chuckled. "Because you're standing at a funny angle."

"I am?" He looked down and then back up at her.

"Did you sleep on the couch?" She glanced over and saw his makeshift bed on the old sofa.

"Yeah, I moved everything out upstairs."

She shook her head. "Your back must be killing you." She took his shoulders and turned him around. "Possibly the worst thing you could do for your back is sleep on that old thing," she said as she started moving her hands over his back. She knew which pressure points to push, which muscles to rub. It wasn't hard to know; after all, his whole left side was a big knot. After a few minutes, she saw his left shoulder lift and his back straighten.

"There." She rubbed his shoulders one last time. "Now you look less like the hunchback of Notre Dame."

He laughed and turned. "Thanks, I think." He rolled his shoulders and neck. She heard a few vertebrae pop back into place. "Wow, I've got to learn that trick." He rolled his shoulders again.

"Now you're ready to work." She smiled and picked up her bag from where she'd dropped it by the door. "I'll just get to work then." She turned to go.

"Holly?" She stopped in the hallway and turned. "Thanks."

She smiled. "No problem."

She spent a few minutes laying out the tarps across the stairs and the hardwood floor in the main entryway. When she moved the large ladder onto it, she stood back and thought about where to start.

The whole entryway to the house was green. There were two large main doors, which she'd never really used since she'd moved into the apartment. She didn't think the doors had been opened in years. Deciding to start on that wall, she opened the first five-gallon pail of paint and used the large stir sticks to mix the color. She tested it on the wall and decided that it would take two coats to completely cover the green.

By lunchtime she had most of the lower walls covered. Travis had walked by several times, carrying large boxes up the stairs. On multiple occasions, she'd helped him carry something up or had just gotten out of his way.

She'd heard him switch on a radio earlier and had enjoyed the old country that flooded the house. She had even sung along on a few of her favorite songs. She took a break and sat on the bottom stair and ate her peanut butter and jelly sandwich and bag of chips for lunch.

After lunch, she opened the front doors to help air out the paint smell and speed up the drying. She started climbing the tall ladder and hauling a small bucket up with her to start on the top half of the area. She painted in long strips with the roller, and then she would move over to the next section and climb the ladder again. It took longer to paint the top half of the entry this way. It was well after dark before she climbed down the ladder for the last time that day. She stood back and looked at her work.

With the second coat of paint, she was going to apply tomorrow, the place would look great. Already it looked more modern and newer.

"Looks great from here," Travis said from the top of the stairs.

She nodded and smiled up at him. "With a second coat tomorrow, you'll have a new home."

He laughed. "At least one that is a lot less green and pink."

She laughed. "How far did you get upstairs?"

"Come on up and see for yourself."

She climbed the stairs and followed him into the bathroom.

Not only had he gotten the new vanity, sink, and toilet in, but he'd started painting over the pink walls.

"I think these walls will need three coats," he said behind her.

"Hmmm." She nodded. "The pink is a lot darker than the green." She walked around and tested the sink. "Did you have to watch videos to learn how to do this?"

He shook his head no. "I helped my dad install the ones in my apartment. He paid to have most of it done, but said I had to learn a few things and showed me how to do all the plumbing."

She smiled. "I always liked your dad. He was the only real father figure I had after my dad died."

"It's funny, after talking to everyone in town, I realize how many lives he touched. I never knew."

"He was the mayor for as long as anyone can remember. He was at every major event." She leaned against the vanity and crossed her arms over her chest as he stood in the doorway. "I can remember him being at every one of my birthday parties." She laughed. "He was even the clown one year when my mother couldn't afford to hire someone to entertain the kids."

"Really?" He shook his head. "I guess I never really appreciated how much he was involved."

She nodded and stood up. "I wish you could have been at his funeral and services. The whole town showed up. So many people had wonderful things to say about him." She wiped a tear from her cheek. "I'm sorry." She wiped more away and started to walk out of the restroom.

"Holly." He stopped her by putting his hands on her shoulders. "I'm sorry about everything." He shook his head.

"What?" She waited and watched him struggle with words.

"About Vegas, about all your stuff." He closed his eyes and dropped his hands from her shoulders.

"Travis, you had nothing to do with either event."

He started to shake his head, and she stopped him by placing her hand on his face. She knew she was splattered with paint but didn't care. "Travis, there is only so much one person can blame themselves."

A burst of laughter escaped his lips. "I'm not the only one who blames me." He took a few steps out of the small room and then turned and looked at her again. "What do you think that was all about?" He threw his hands towards the back wall. "The mess in your apartment. That was a warning. To me!" His voice rose.

She frowned at him. "I don't understand."

He ran his hands through his hair and then dropped his arms to his side. "Savannah. She stopped by again the other night. She demanded that I step up and tell the town that I'm the father." He shook his head and closed his eyes.

Holly laughed. "I had a run in with her yesterday before I went riding."

His eyes flew open, and anger burned in them. "Are you okay?" He looked over her.

She laughed. "I know how to handle myself. Remember, I'm the one that broke her nose a few months ago."

He nodded, and she saw him relax a little.

"She said a lot of things." She shook her head and stepped out into the hallway. "She kept trying to convince me that you were the father. She…" She looked down at her hands and scraped the dry paint off the back of her thumb.

"What?" He stepped towards her and put his fingers under her chin, nudging it up until she looked at him.

"She told me you'd tire of me soon enough." She shook her head until his fingers dropped from her skin.

"She lied." Her eyes flew back to his, waiting. "I don't think I could tire of you." He closed his eyes and stepped back. "That's the problem." When he looked at her again, she searched his eyes. "I can't do this. I don't want to." He turned and took a few steps until she stopped him with a hand on his.

"Travis, there's nothing you can do to make this go away. Not now."

He laughed. "I just need to be myself and you'll see for yourself soon enough." He jerked his arm free of hers and took off.

She stood in the hallway and watched him go down the stairs and out the front door. She stood there for a few moments before she walked back downstairs and started cleaning up the paint brushes in the laundry room sink. When she'd closed everything up again for the night, she walked back to her apartment and took the hottest shower her skin would tolerate.

Her eyes and nose were red when she looked at herself in the mirror. She combed her long hair and thought about everything he'd said. How would she convince him that he was no longer the troublemaker he used to be? If he didn't believe it, then she'd just have to show him.

When she finally lay down, she dreamed of Travis holding her. Of how good it would feel to have his hands on her again.

Travis walked to the end of the block and when he still felt bad, he continued to walk farther. Even when the streetlights stopped, he walked and walked.

Why couldn't Holly—and the whole town of Fairplay, for that matter—let him be? He hadn't planned on coming back, hadn't planned on staying.

Something inside of him told him to run from the town and in the last few years, he'd learned to listen to his inner voice. He'd spent years ignoring it and look at where that had gotten him.

He thought of his mother and his stomach turned. Did she even have a little voice inside? He hadn't talked to her or seen her since that night four years ago when the sheriff had cuffed her and put her into the back of his car. She'd screamed her confession loud enough for him to hear it as he'd watched.

He looked around and realized he'd walked to the new park. The new playground stood in the bright lights for the safety of any kids or teenagers who wanted to hang out after dark. He walked over and sat on the swing, pushing it a little as he remembered his mother. Did she know that his dad had died? He was sure someone would have told her at the facility she was in. She'd been moved to a state-run place less than an hour away. He must have driven by the place a thousand times when he'd gone into Houston to party.

She'd gotten off easy for what she'd done. Guilty of attempted murder and all she'd received was twenty years in a psych ward. He leaned his head on the cool chain and wished more than anything that his father was there to guide him.

His dad had always known what to do. He opened his eyes and looked around the park. Maybe this was his father's way of telling him what to do with his future.

He loved designing and overseeing construction. All he would need was another year or two at school and he could earn his degree. Maybe he'd find someplace to start a business then. Maybe he'd build and design new homes. He liked knowing that families would enjoy the spaces he created.

He stood up from the swing and looked around the dark park and smiled. He'd include parks and old theaters in his work list. He'd enjoyed seeing the old place come together and couldn't wait until all the work was finished, making the theater what it used to be. No, better than it used to be.

He started walking back to his house and this time as he went, he noticed the homes and business he passed as he went. Some of them had been updated, others were in dire need of repair or replacement. He knew that some of the townspeople had abandoned their homes after the tornado. Some had chosen to take the insurance money and leave, and others had stuck it out and fixed what they could when they could.

There was still a lot of work to be done in Fairplay, and he knew his father would have wanted the town to be returned to its former glory. He could do it. Maybe he'd stick around here and finish what his father had started.

He turned onto his street and saw the light in the apartment above the garage. Maybe he could be good enough for Holly.

He was just outside his house when he heard the vehicle turn down the quiet road. He turned and saw Billy's truck. When it turned into his driveway, he sighed.

"Hey, Travis." Billy was alone this time and Travis watched as he stepped out of the truck. He could tell that his friend was wasted and probably a little high.

"Hi, Billy. Should you be driving?" He held his friend upright so he wouldn't fall face first into the cement.

Billy laughed. "Sure, I'm fine." He waved his hand and pushed Travis' hands away. "I was just heading up to the cabin for the weekend. Thought I'd check and see if you wanted to tag along."

"I won't be partying with you anymore." He shoved his hands in his pocket. "I've kind of outgrown all that."

Billy sneered. "Corey kept telling me you were too high and mighty to hang with your bros anymore." Billy leaned against his truck. "I should've listened to him."

"Why don't you come in, I'll make some coffee and get you something to eat." He reached for his friend's arm. Billy threw his hand off and leaned away.

"I don't need your help." He stumbled a little. "You come back into town and act like you don't know us. Like you aren't one of us," he yelled. "You'll always be one of us. You think just because your old man died and left you all this"—he waved towards the house— "that you aren't one of us. Well, you'll remember soon enough." He laughed and walked around his truck.

"Billy, you shouldn't be driving." He stopped his friend from getting into the driver's side. Billy swung out and clocked him in the jaw. "Damn it. I'm trying to help you." Travis held his jaw.

"I don't need your help. I don't need anyone's help." His chest puffed up. "You think I haven't heard what everyone's saying about me? That Billy Jackson, he'll end up killing himself or someone else. That Billy Jackson won't amount to anything. He'll turn out just like his old man."

Travis remembered now that Billy's father was serving life in the state pen for beating a man to death in a bar fight.

"Billy, everyone can change. Look at me." He looked down at his feet. "Look at my family. Does that mean I'll end up like my mother?"

Billy stopped and looked at him, then shook his head no. "You're nothing like your old lady."

Travis nodded. At least he had that.

"Why don't you come in and sleep it off. I've got some of Jamella's apple pie left in the fridge."

"Really?" Billy looked off towards the house. "What about her?" He nodded towards the garage.

Travis looked and saw Holly standing at the top of the stairs.

"She's staying at the apartment. I'm in the big house for now."

"Oh, shit. Really?" Billy looked towards the garage and back towards him.

"Billy?" Travis took a step towards him, already reading the guilt on his friend's face.

"We thought. That is…Savannah said…"

"What did you do?" He took his friend's arm.

"Shit." Billy yanked his arm away.

"It was you, wasn't it? You broke into the apartment and destroyed Holly's stuff."

"We didn't break in. We still had the key you gave us. Besides, it was all Savannah's idea. She's the one that said you'd tossed her out and was shacking up with the book woman."

"Why?" It was Holly that asked from just behind him. He dropped Billy's arm and stepped back to take hers. "Why did you trash it?"

"We thought Travis was staying there."

"I heard. Why did you break in and ruin what you thought was your friend's stuff?"

She stepped around him and went face to face with almost two hundred pounds of drunken Billy.

Billy shrugged his shoulders and looked down at his feet. "It seemed the thing to do after Travis started acting like we were scum."

"What?" he asked, stepping closer. "I never treated you like you were scum."

"Sure you did. You wouldn't hang out with us and every time you saw us, you had this funny look on your face like you smelled something bad."

Travis thought about it. "I didn't mean to treat you bad. It's hard for me." He dropped his hands. "I don't want to go back to being bad boy Travis Nolan."

Billy laughed. "You'll always be bad boy Travis Nolan. You're the one that taught us how to shoot, how to smoke, gave me my first beer." He shook his head. "Hell, the whole town saw your ass when we streaked during the homecoming game our senior year." Billy laughed.

Travis laughed and slapped his friend on the shoulder. "Good ol' times." Then he sobered. "But for me, they have to be in the past. I don't want to be the same kid I used to be."

Billy looked down at his feet. "Hell, I know I have to shape up." He looked up at Travis and his eyes sparkled. "I've got my own kid on the way. She's due any day now."

"What?" Travis looked at his friend and smiled. "Well, hell. I didn't know you'd shacked up with someone special."

Billy looked down again. "I meant to tell you." Then he glanced up. "Course she's telling everyone in town the baby is yours."

Travis gasped. "Savannah? Savannah's baby?"

Billy smiled and nodded. "I know you two used to have a thing. But, well, after you left town we sorta hooked up."

Travis laughed. "Of course, you did."

"She found out about the baby and freaked, then ran off to Vegas to find you."

Travis took his friends shoulders and walked with him into the house. Holly followed.

"Well, I guess you deserve that piece of pie now. You're going to be a dad."

Billy smiled and nodded. "I guess I'll take it." He stopped just before walking into the back door and turned to Holly. "I'm really sorry about your stuff. Honest, we only meant to punk him for ditching us."

Holly smiled. "It's okay, no real harm was done."

Travis looked at her and felt something shift in his chest. "Holly, why don't you help me make some coffee?"

She nodded and followed them inside. Travis pushed his friend gently onto the couch.

"I know I have to clean up," Billy said, running his

hands through his hair. "Honest, I was on the path before Savannah started telling everyone you were the father. I guess it just set me off. I even tried to make her jealous by going out with other women. God, I love that woman." Billy rested his head into his hands and sighed.

"I'll get the pie and make some coffee." Holly said and walked into the kitchen.

CHAPTER 14

She didn't know what had changed in Travis, but over the next few days, he acted like a huge weight had been lifted from him. He rushed around the house and finished everything that had needed to be done there. They talked about her store and apartment more often, and he actually seemed excited to see the final product.

They were days away from getting the certificate of occupancy on her apartment, so she could move back in. Travis had even hung out with Billy and Corey a few nights at the house. He'd cooked out and they'd played poker until one in the morning. It was nice that the other men didn't complain that alcohol and smoking weren't allowed.

Billy had confessed that he'd caught Savannah smoking and had threatened to take the baby away once it was born if she didn't stop. He told them how they'd stopped smoking together. He showed Travis that he was wearing one of the patches and occasionally popped a nicotine gum into his mouth.

She wondered if Travis had had as hard a time quitting as Billy was having. She had stuck around for a while, but when it was apparent that everyone was getting tired of her winning, she walked up to her apartment and called it a night, leaving the men alone.

She heard them laughing and jumping in the pool around one but then drifted off, dreaming of Travis holding her again.

The next morning, she showed up early to the store. Instead of walking around downstairs, she headed upstairs to her apartment. There were just a few minor things left to do. She'd spent two days here painting a warm taupe in the living areas and a soft honey color in her bedroom and bathroom.

She was getting pretty tired of being patient with Travis. She kept telling herself that it was better this way. He was going to be moving in a few short months, and she needed to focus on restarting her business. Besides, she had a lot to do with the new aspects of her bookstore.

She'd spent some of her spare time going through wine lists and trying new coffees that she planned on serving.

She had found several new recipes to try for baked goods. She had even baked a few and had handed them out to the construction workers who all begged her to bring more.

Today she'd brought a cranberry coffee crumble cake. She hadn't even had time to taste it herself before leaving that morning. She had set it on the bar downstairs with plates and forks and a large thermos of French vanilla coffee.

She walked around and made a mental list of items that would need to be addressed. The wood blinds would need to be hung after all of the windowsills had been finished. All of the doors needed stoppers on them, and the bathtub wasn't draining properly. Most likely it was clogged up with the dried paint she'd accidentally dumped down it. The ceiling fans still needed to be installed, and the vent above the stove was still sitting on the floor.

She leaned against the new countertop and sighed. She'd started thinking about living in another place. One where the kitchen was wide and open and overlooked a swimming pool and a garage with a mother-in-law apartment above it. One where she would walk in and see Travis standing in his jeans with no shirt or shoes. One where he would be there every day, waiting for her.

She closed her eyes and talked herself out of dreaming about something that could never be.

"If you keep feeding the men like this, they'll never get back to work."

She opened her eyes and saw Travis standing in front of her, a plate of cranberry cake balanced on a cup of steaming coffee.

"They deserve it." She pasted on a smile and motioned around. "Just look at how wonderful this looks."

He looked around and smiled. "It did come together pretty well." Then he looked at her and his smile fell away. "Are you okay?"

She nodded and turned away from him to hide the sadness in her eyes. "Just thinking about all the wonderful times I'll have here. Roger tells me I can start moving in on Monday."

"Monday?" She turned and saw him frowning.

She nodded. "It'll be nice to get my stuff out of storage and sleep in my own bed again."

He looked down at the cake and then sat it on the counter, forgotten. "If you need any help…" he said, avoiding her eyes.

"Thanks, but I've already enlisted Reece and Grant. I don't have too many heavy items. I think they can handle it." She folded her hands behind her back.

"It sounds like downstairs will be ready in a few weeks."

She nodded. "I'll have a lot more to move in there than here." She smiled and looked around. "Actually, I may need an army to help me move it all back in."

"Well, I'd be happy to help."

She looked over at him and nodded. "I'll take it." She turned and walked into the living room. "How's Billy doing?"

Travis picked up his plate and coffee. "He's hanging in there. Corey…" He shook his head. "Well, Corey isn't slowing down. But I can tell that Billy is really trying."

She nodded. She'd seen the same thing. Having a kid on the way had really changed Billy. Especially since everyone in town now knew that Savannah's kid was his.

Savannah's parents were forcing them to marry and a very large wedding was planned for a few months after the baby was due to arrive.

"It sure makes a difference when there's a kid involved," she said, absentmindedly.

"Yeah, I guess so." He stopped and looked down at her. "Have you ever thought of having one? A kid that is?"

She almost fell over, and he reached his free hand out and steadied her. "Um, sure. I guess so. I wouldn't just want one though," she said, opening the door so he could step out. "I was an only child and wouldn't want my son or daughter to be as lonely as I was."

He nodded. "I often wished I had a little brother or sister. Someone I could blame for things I did." He smiled and she laughed.

"I was always jealous of Haley's sisters. The close bond they have."

He nodded. "Yeah, when I was with Alex it was hell sneaking past them." He laughed. "Especially Haley." He shook his head. "Man, do I owe that woman some apologies."

"Oh?" She stopped at the bottom of the stairs.

He chuckled. "Yeah. Let's just say I'm glad bad Travis isn't around anymore. I hear her husband is the new law in town."

She laughed and nodded. "Wes is on the force now. I hear he's next in line when the sheriff finally decides to retire."

Travis laughed. "I guess I'll have to stop by and make sure I get on his good side. I haven't run into him since I've been back."

"Well, they're pretty busy. They have twin boys now."

He shook his head and smiled. "You know; I can remember hanging out at their place when I was a kid. Their father would take us riding. I haven't been on the back of a horse in too long."

She smiled. "If you want, you can go with me sometime."

His eyebrows shot up. "I'd like that. Actually, maybe you can help me out with another matter."

"Sure." She walked over to the bar and took a plate and grabbed one of the last pieces of cranberry cake.

"I'll be having a huge garage sale in few weeks. I have no idea what everything is worth or how to go about having a garage sale." He leaned against the counter and nibbled on his cake.

"I can help." She smiled and took a bite of her cake.

"Oh, my goodness," he said, looking down at his plate. "This is the best thing I've ever had."

She nodded, and her smile fell away. "Had I known it was going to be this good, I would have kept it all to myself." She smiled and took another bite.

The rest of the day, Travis thought about how he'd reacted when he'd heard Holly would be moving out of the apartment above the garage soon. He'd gotten used to her being there every evening when he got home. Even if he hadn't seen her, he always looked for the lights and got a warm feeling when he'd see them on.

He'd been doing a lot of thinking since Billy had started hanging around. He could see positive changes in his friend. They had started running together every other day. Travis knew he didn't need to train as much as he had when he'd been cage fighting, but the workouts helped clear his mind and allowed him to focus more.

He'd finished everything inside and the appraiser had finally come to put a price tag on the place. The "for sale" sign had sat out front of the house for the last few days. He couldn't believe how much his father's assets were worth.

Once everything sold, he'd have enough to start all

over somewhere else. He would have enough money to attend school wherever he wanted. As he sat down that night to look at schools online, his mind kept coming back to how sad Holly had looked that morning.

He knew he was doing the best thing for her by staying away from her. They'd even created somewhat of a friendship, something he didn't feel like he had with any of his other exes.

Savannah had steered clear of him. Even though Billy had assured him that she was busy getting ready for the baby and wedding, he doubted he'd heard the last from her.

Alex had smiled and been polite to him every time he'd seen her, but he hadn't worked up enough nerve to actually talk to her, not after what his mother had done to her and her husband.

He knew he needed to bury the hatchet with her and Grant, but he just couldn't bring himself to step up yet. One night when he'd been going to Mama's, he'd seen Alex and her family sitting in the diner laughing, and he'd walked home and eaten a peanut butter and jelly sandwich instead. He knew it was chicken of him, but he just wasn't ready. He had a stop to make first. He needed to make the hour drive up to see his mother before he left town for good.

The next day he woke up and dressed in his finest suit. When he walked outside, instead of getting into his silver Hyundai, he uncovered the Mustang and walked into the garage to retrieve the keys. When he came back out, Holly was standing there in a pretty sundress.

"Going for a drive?"

He nodded. "Going to church?"

She looked down at her dress. "Yes, they have a luncheon every Sunday that I've been avoiding for a while."

He looked at her. "What do you say you avoid it for another day?"

She looked up at him. "I'd love to." She smiled as he walked over and opened the passenger side.

"I'll warn you, I'm heading up to visit my mother." He saw her step falter. Then she laughed.

"It's still preferable to listening to a bunch of mothers talk about how perfect their kids are as they run around screaming and getting dirty."

He smiled and nodded. "You may be singing a different tune on the drive home."

She smiled. "Can we have the top down? I have a scarf." She pulled a scarf out of her bag and started to tie her hair up.

He laughed. "Why not." He flipped the locks on the old top and pushed it down. He had to admit, the car drove like a dream as he pulled out of town. They saw several people driving into town on their way out. Holly waved and smiled at each one she recognized.

"Tell me you're not going to sell this beauty." She turned to him.

"I wasn't going to. Actually, I'd thought of selling my Hyundai and taking this one for myself."

She smiled. "You should. After all the work you've done on it." She rubbed her hands over the leather interior. "Besides, I'll bet it runs better than the Hyundai."

He nodded. "It does so far."

He really enjoyed the power the old car had, and when he hit the highway, he opened the car up to see how it handled and was happily surprised that it still felt like it was gliding across the pavement when it hit top speed.

"I saw that the sign in front of the house was gone. Did you sell the house?"

He glanced over at her without saying a word.

She frowned. "It's such a nice place. It deserves a young family with kids and dogs."

"Dogs?" He looked over at her.

"Sure. I always wanted brothers or sisters and dogs." She looked over at him. "Didn't you want pets?"

There had been a time when he'd asked for a puppy for Christmas, but his mother was anti-pets, and he'd stopped asking once she'd explained that animals wrecked the house.

"I guess so. It would have never been allowed and so I stopped asking. What kind of dog?" He looked over at her.

"I always wanted a beagle. They're so cute when they're little." She smiled, and he couldn't stop himself from living in her dream as she continued to talk about it.

When they drove up to the state-run facility less than an hour later, his mood had changed. He'd been so nervous about his visit with his mother but talking to Holly during the drive had washed away all his nerves and replaced it with an inner peace. He couldn't explain the change fully.

He parked the car and helped her out. She removed her scarf and shook her hair back into place. It looked perfect. She looked perfect.

"Here." She reached up and ran her hands through his hair. "You need a haircut." She smiled as she straightened his hair.

"Yeah." He frowned, instantly thinking about what his

mother would say. She'd always gotten on his case about growing his hair too long. "I suppose I should have…"

"You'll be fine. You look very handsome." She took his hand. "If you want, I'll stay out here?"

He shook his head. "No, I'd rather not go it alone."

She nodded. "I always got along with your mother. Your folks were my godparents, you know."

"So you said." He smiled down at her and squeezed her hand.

They checked in at the main desk where the nurse informed him which room his mother was in. When they walked up the stairs, he couldn't control the shaking he felt. She must have picked up on it because her hand tightened around his.

He knocked on the door and his mother opened it. She looked a lot thinner. She must have lost fifty pounds. Her hair had turned from a warm blonde to a dark gray. There were new lines under her eyes and she wore no makeup.

"Travis?" Her eyes lit up. "Is that you?" She reached out and grabbed him. "Oh, my baby has come back to me." She pulled him into a hug and memories flooded his mind. His arms went around the woman whose only sin, other than trying to commit murder, had been trying to give her son everything he'd ever desired.

CHAPTER 15

*H*olly stood back in the hallway and watched Travis engulf his mother in his arms. She saw his mother's eyes light up when she saw her standing behind him.

"Holly Bridles? Oh, this is a treat. Come on in you two." She walked over and hugged her quickly then motioned for them to walk into her small room. There was a single bed against one wall, a small kitchen area, and a large flat-screen television on the wall, which had been put on mute.

"How are they treating you here, Mom?" Travis asked as he walked in, looking around.

"Oh, you know how it is." She looked at him and smiled. "They think I'm crazy." She smiled at Holly who smiled back. "They won't let me have knives or glass or other sharp objects." She held up a cup with tea in it. "Plastic." She shook her head. "Your father would have a fit if he knew I was forced to eat off of something more suitable for picnics." She sat down and glanced towards the television again. "But other than that, I'm having a blast. I get to play Bingo every Tuesday night. Cards are two times a week and we have arts and crafts on Fridays. There's even a movie night." She said all this while keeping her eyes on the television set.

"Mom," Travis said and waited until his mother turned her eyes back to him. "I don't know if someone has told you." He reached across the table and looked at their joined hands. Holly stood inside the doorway, not wanting to make a move. "Dad died a few months ago."

His mother glanced at him. "Oh, they told me alright. Lies." She shook her head. "Can you believe it? We'll have a good laugh about it when I get out of here."

"Mother—" he started again, but she started talking about something else. The conversation kept turning weirder and less than a half an hour later, she asked them to leave so she could watch her show.

"I never miss Jeopardy," she said, patting Holly's hand. "Roy always gets the answers right, but since he's back home I'll have to guess them all myself." She smiled and hugged Travis' mother. "Now, you tell your mother 'hi' for me. Katie was one of my best friends, you know."

Holly nodded. She'd known that her mother and Travis' mom had been friends for a while. That's how they had ended up being her godparents.

"Mom," Travis said, taking her attention. "Are you sure you don't need anything?"

"Oh, no. I'm fine. Anything I need, all I have to do is ask." She patted her son's arm while her eyes darted to the set. "Now, you tell your father to come up here and visit me. I haven't seen him for a while."

He nodded, and she watched some of the color leave his face.

When they walked outside, the heat of the day hit them full force.

"Would you mind if we went for a drive?" he asked, sitting behind the wheel.

"I'd love to." She tied the scarf around her hair again and tucked the long strands behind her glasses, so they wouldn't fly in her face.

"We can grab some food first if you want."

She nodded. "There's a small place just there." She pointed across the street to a small family diner.

It wasn't as cozy as Mama's, but the food was tolerable. They ate in silence, and she couldn't help but notice that his mood had changed.

They left the diner and drove down the winding back roads that would eventually lead them to Fairplay. She enjoyed the cool breeze on her face and the silence in the air as the tall pines flew by them.

When he pulled off a side road, she didn't complain, knowing it led up to a point where you could overlook a large river and field just outside of town. As the car climbed the back roads. She rested her head against the headrest.

He pulled the car to a stop a few feet from the overlook and turned off the engine.

"She's the same," he said, still looking at the view. "I had thought…" He swallowed. "I thought she would have changed, become crazier somehow."

Holly looked over at him and tried not to show her feelings.

"Other than thinking Dad is still alive…I guess I

always knew there was something off about her growing up. I've just been in denial." He shook his head and glanced over at her.

"She loves you." She smiled. "I wasn't that close with her. I know that most everyone in town still thinks of her fondly."

He laughed and shook his head. "You know, I've heard that Alex and her sisters have visited her."

Holly smiled. "I would have been surprised if they hadn't. I've been there myself."

"You?" He turned and looked at her. "You've been there before today?"

She nodded. "My mother came up to visit shortly after she was moved there. We bought her the bed and television. They used to be best friends."

He nodded and brushed the scarf off her head. "You've messed up your hair." He used his fingers to tame it. She knew it was a helpless case but didn't care since she was enjoying the cool breeze and the crisp night air. "I love the feel of it." He was looking at her hair as his fingers brushed it away from her face. She closed her eyes, wishing that he would never stop.

"I'm glad you came with me today." He leaned closer to her and she held her breath as his lips touched hers. The kiss was different than before. It was slow and soft and spoke of promises that would come.

When he pulled her closer to him, she went willingly and wrapped her arms around his neck. She'd missed the feeling of him, his sweet taste, the smell of him next to her. As he pulled back, she looked up into his dark eyes and felt her heart melt.

"Holly…" He brushed a wild strand of her hair that

had gotten caught in the night air. "There's no guarantee that I won't end up nuts like my mother."

She shook her head and laughed. "Every family has a crazy person. My uncle thinks he's the lost heir to the Hearst fortune." She smiled.

She watched his lips curl into a smile. "I've finally decided what I'm going to do." He leaned back and tucked her close to his shoulder. She rested her head there and watched the sun sink lower, casting hues of purple and bright pinks across the night sky.

"Oh?"

He nodded. "I'm going to go to school."

She felt her heart sink. Here he was, holding her in his arms and talking about leaving again. She wanted to smack him, but instead, she closed her eyes as tears threatened to escape.

"I figure I can earn my degree in less than two years since I have most of my basic credits out of the way thanks to my dad's persistence." He chuckled. "Then I plan on using my inheritance to start my own construction company. I'll do it all. Design, build and sell. I think I'll start with a small housing project." He wrapped his arm tighter around her when she shivered. She didn't want to tell him she wasn't cold, but she just couldn't bring herself to say anything just yet. "I know these are all just plans, but I was kind of hoping…" He pulled back and lifted her chin until she looked up into his eyes. "I was hoping you'd take a chance on me, anyway."

She blinked a few times. His dark eyes searched hers. "Travis?" She licked her lips, unsure of what it was he was saying.

"I'd like to stay in Fairplay, take online classes, open a

business, and live in my parents' house with you. I'd like to get a dog—no—make it *two* dogs. We wouldn't want them to get lonely." He smiled and cupped her face. "I'd like to raise a couple kids as well." He smiled. "If you'll have me and my crazy past."

She blinked and swallowed. "Of course, I will." She smiled.

"Holly, there's just one more thing." He pulled her closer and looked deep into her eyes. "I love you. I want to be with you for the rest of my life. Only you." He waited.

"I love you, too. Only you." She smiled and pulled his head down to hers and kissed him.

*T*ravis stood outside of the store and helped cut the blue ribbon. Cheers rose up and he reached across and pulled Holly down into a deep kiss, only to hear more cheers.

When he pulled back, she was smiling up at him. "Shall we open up for business?"

He nodded and pulled her back upright. "Holly's is now open for business," he called out to the crowd.

They walked into the new store hand in hand, and he stopped at the threshold and kissed her again. "For luck," he said to the crowd before they flooded the store. They all laughed.

He stood back, and Holly and her new employees busied themselves with taking orders and helping customers. There was a band playing softly on the stage near the back as people grabbed seats and enjoyed their desserts and drinks.

He'd grabbed a seat near the front, so he could watch

Holly as she worked. It still got to him how much energy she had.

"It looks like Holly's is a success." He looked up to see Alex and Grant standing in front of his table. He stood and nodded.

"Looks like it." He looked at his shoes, something he had done around them since his return.

"We just wanted to tell you," Alex said, reaching out and taking his hand, "that we don't blame you." He looked up quickly into both of their eyes. Alex smiled, and he remembered all the good times they'd had together. Gone were all the bad memories, all the horrors he'd caused her.

"I have this," Grant said, pulling out a letter and handing it to him. "It's from your dad. He wanted me to give it to you on opening day." He nodded around to the crowd.

When Travis reached out and took it, Grant held his hand out for him to shake. He hesitated for a second, then looked into his eyes and saw no hard feelings and shook the man's hand without remorse.

"You found yourself a good man," he said, looking over to Alex, who laughed.

"Yeah, go figure." She smiled and held onto her husband. "You've got a pretty sweet treat." She nodded towards Holly. "Don't let that one get away from you."

He smiled. "She's mine for life, as soon as we can plan it."

They smiled and nodded then walked over to where their family sat near the stage.

He sat down and looked at the envelope in his hands. Flipping it over, he opened it and pulled out the note.

Travis,

Thank you. You don't know how much it means to me knowing that you've grown into the man I always knew you would be. There's more than one reason I started this project and if everything has gone according to my dreams, you know the reason I chose the bookstore.

Healing takes place on so many different levels. Holly has and will always be the daughter we never had. When I started this project a few days ago, I got word from my doctor that I had an inoperable brain aneurysm. Son, I want you to know that I wouldn't have changed a thing, except to have you by my side and hold you one last time.

You've made me the proudest man on Earth and in heaven.

p.s. Stop by and see your mother sometime. She may be off, but she loves you.

Never forget that I love you.

When he looked up from the letter, he felt tears slip down his face. Then Holly was there holding him, and he knew that he was right where he belonged.

PROLOGUE

Ryan jumped back as he watched a dozen dark figures flood out of the cemetery. He was tackled from behind and hit the ground with a groan as his hands were yanked behind his head. Shouts and screams could be heard over his head as he felt cold metal slap around his wrists.

"You're in a lot of trouble, son." Someone said over him. When he tried to turn his head to see who was talking, his face was shoved back into the dirt. "Don't move until I say so." He was quickly frisked, then pulled to his feet.

He shook the dirt from his face and looked around the old cemetery. He'd come out here to drink his problems away with a six pack of the cheapest beer he could get his hands on. He'd barely started the first beer and now he watched as his beer spilled out into the ground.

"I didn't do anything," he insisted the second he stood up.

The heavy police officer laughed. "The hell you didn't." He got in his face. "Where's Roberts?"

"Who?" Ryan looked at the older man.

"Don't play games with me, son. We know you set up a meeting tonight to meet him. So, where is he?"

"Listen, you've got the wrong guy," Ryan started to say, only to be yanked back a foot by the cop holding him.

"You'd best think long and hard about your answer. It could mean the difference between life in prison and life in prison." He laughed.

"Listen, I just came out here to drink and forget about my old man beating up on me." He nodded to the broken bottles the police officer was now standing on.

The man looked down at his feet and shook his head. "I guess we'll have to haul you in and see if we can get some answers out of you then."

Ryan was shoved in the back of an unmarked police car and driven out of his small town. As he watched the lights disappear, he wondered if he'd been destined to always be in trouble.

ROPING RYAN

CHAPTER 1

*T*en years later...

Nikki applied another layer of red lipstick to her lips and made sure her breasts stuck out just far enough to get the attention she was hoping for. She looked across the room at her mark and took a deep breath to steady her nerves.

He was sexier than the last man she'd hunted down. If it wasn't for his long dark hair, the rough beard he had on his face, and the flashy clothes he was wearing, he would have been her type.

He'd been harder to find than most. She'd been watching this one for almost three days and had lost him until she'd had a lead from one of her regular snitches.

The bar wasn't her style. The music was too loud, the clothes too small, and the drugs that went in and out of the place scared most people away. She tucked her small clutch purse under her arm. She knew how to protect herself.

She pasted on her best slutty smile and walked across

the floor towards her man. She saw the second his eyes zeroed in on her, the moment desire flashed in his green eyes, and she knew she'd found her mark.

"Well, hello," she purred and waited until he asked her to sit. But instead of him motioning for her to take the empty spot, he glanced around and quickly said.

"Not now. Come back in ten minutes, okay babe."

She pouted and sat down anyway. "Oh, what if I don't want to wait? There are a lot of other fish in this bar." She giggled and swung her arm over his shoulders and started to play with his long dark hair, wrapping it around her fingers playfully.

She felt him tense but relax a little as she rubbed her breast against his shoulder. She knew how to work it, especially when so much was on the line.

"Listen, I'd love to…entertain you, but I have a meeting I've got to…" He stopped when three men dressed in nice suits walked over and stood by them.

"What's this?" one of them said, looking at her.

"Ditch the ho," the other said, sitting down across from them.

She pouted and looked towards her mark. "Come on baby, let's get out of here." She started to tug on his arm, but he stopped her.

"She just sat down and now she's leaving." He pushed her off of him. She stood up and put her hands on her hips and looked down at him.

"Jerk." She turned on her heels and walked back to the bar, pretending to be hurt. She sat back along the side of the bar where they were unable to see her and watched the four men while thinking of her next move.

Several men approached her, asking if they could buy

her drinks. She turned them all down and sipped her water with lime.

She watched the men arguing and when they all stood and walked towards the back exit, she saw her chance and followed. She wasn't going to lose him again.

When she stepped out into the alley with her drink in hand, she wobbled a little and purposely fell into one of the men. Looking up, she froze when she realized what was happening.

Her mark stood across from her, held up by two of the other men. Fresh blood dripped down his face and she could see his lip and eyes swelling.

"Hey," she said, putting a little drunken slur in. "Is this a robbery?" She leaned against the man who she'd bumped into. When she felt the gun in his inside pocket she tried not to show her irritation. Damn, this was going to get complicated.

"Bitch." The man pushed her away. "Is this your ho?" He pulled her arm up and away from his jacket.

Her mark shook his head and grunted when he was hit in the ribs quickly and released by the two men.

"Get rid of them," the leader said, pushing her across the small alley into her mark's arms. The man turned and walked back into the nightclub.

When the two men started walking towards them, Nikki pulled her gun out from her purse and pointed it at the men.

"Freeze," she said, holding the weapon at their chests. They both stopped, looked at the gun and, then at her and laughed.

"Look, the little lady has a little gun," the men said, pulling bigger guns from their coats.

"Got anything bigger in that bag of yours?" her mark asked. When she shook her head, he whispered, "Looks like we'll have to make a run for it." He grabbed the gun from her fingers, released two shots in the direction of the men, grabbed her arm in a death grip, and took off running down the alley.

She tried to keep up, but the sexy heels she'd worn were slowing her down. She could hear the men gaining on them, and she pulled on her arm until the man stopped yanking her down the back streets.

"Here." She pulled him down a side alley and yanked open the door to her planned get-a-way route. Then leaned against the doorway and closed her eyes, listening to see if they had escaped the chase.

"How did you know this was here?" he whispered after they heard the men run past their hiding spot.

"I've used this place a few times." She reached down and removed her shoes. Her feet were killing her and would most likely be swollen for the next few days. She hated wearing heels. When she looked up, she smiled. "Can I have my gun back, sweetie?"

He looked at her and shook his head no. "Not until you tell me why you've been following me." He held the weapon up and pointed it at her.

She pouted. "Don't flatter yourself. I saw you at the bar and thought you looked like a good time."

He shook his head. "Try a different story. I first noticed you outside my hotel three days ago."

She looked at him blankly.

"Then at the bus stop yesterday. You were wearing a long tan coat and tall black boots." He leaned against the other wall and wiped the blood from his lip.

"I think you have me confused with someone else." She took a step closer and watched him lift the gun back up.

She sighed and leaned back against the door. "I guess I just like the look of you."

He chuckled. "Was it Carlton? Who do you work for?"

She blinked a few times and sighed. "I don't know who Carlton is."

"Then who hired you?" He held the gun up and took a step closer to her.

"Your brother. Reece West. I was hired to find you and take you back to your brother."

"Reece?" Ryan took a step back and shook his head in disbelief. He remembered the last time he had seen his twin brother. "Reece hired you?"

She nodded and held out her hand for the weapon. "Can I have my gun back?"

He shook his head again. "You've just blown three years of hard work in under five minutes." He about everything that had just happened.

His brother was looking for him and because of this woman, his contacts wouldn't trust him anymore. Not only that, they'd most likely be watching out for him and probably take out a hit on him. Damn, he'd have to report back to his chief. He might even have to find a place to lay low for a while, at least until they could finally find Dante, the man he'd spent the last three years looking for. He'd been so close. Tonight's meeting was the last in a long line of meetings to get closer to him.

He had been told he was going to be taken to the man. That was the only reason he'd walked out of the back of the club with the three men earlier. He felt his stomach roll. Damn. This wasn't going to look good on his record.

He turned back to her. "You said my brother sent you?"

She nodded and crossed her arms over her chest. He'd only noticed that she'd been following him the first time because of her looks. She was tall with dark hair, killer blue eyes, and sexy red-hot lips. Even in the slutty outfit, she wore tonight, he couldn't help but admire how classy she looked. Upscale, he'd thought the first time he saw her. She hadn't belonged in that scummy neighborhood in downtown Houston. Nor had she belonged in the loud club tonight. She belonged in a fine restaurant with a glass of champagne in her hands.

"Who are you?" He took a step towards her.

She sighed and glared at him. "I've already told you. Your brother—"

"Your name, princess," he interrupted.

"I don't see as that's any of your—"

He waved the gun. "It is while I'm holding this." He smiled.

"Nikki."

"Nikki?" He waited.

She sighed again. "Nikki Dawson."

"Why would my brother hire you?"

She looked down at the gun and closed her pretty red lips. "I won't answer any more until I have my gun back."

He chuckled. "Then we're in for a very long and quiet night." He took her hand and started walking into the dark room. "At least tell me if there's a back door to this place."

"Over there." She pointed towards the side. "My car is just—"

"Good, give me the keys," he interrupted again. They didn't have time for stories, not now.

She yanked her arm away from him. "You may have my gun, but what makes you think I'll give you the keys to my car?"

"Because, princess, you've just pissed off one of the biggest and baddest drug lords there is and if you think he's going to let our little vanishing act get past him, you're sorely mistaken." He reached over and took her arm again.

"Drug lords?" A cute little line appeared between her eyebrows. "What were you doing with those kinds of men?" She glanced over her shoulder and he watched her shiver.

"I was working," he said, opening the heavy door a crack and glancing around. "Which car is yours?"

"The silver Honda," she said pointing to the last of a long row of cars parked along the curb.

"Good. Now the keys?" He held out his hand and waited. She looked up at him for a moment, the pulled the keys out of her purse. "Good, now when I say so, we run to the car as fast as you can. Got it?"

She nodded and held her shoes and purse closer to her chest. He reached down and took her hand. When they were less than ten feet from her car, he felt the first bullet whiz by his left hear. He shoved her down as they ducked behind a car. "Damn." He looked around for a better route. "We're going to have to crawl." He looked down at her short dress and frowned at the new scratches she had on those lovely knees.

"Lead the way." She motioned for him to move. He had to admire her guts and the fact that she wasn't complaining about crawling on the hard ground.

He took her hand and started ducking behind the cars. When they finally made it to the passenger side of her car, he opened it and jumped in, making sure she stayed low when she ducked in behind him.

He popped the keys in the ignition quickly and hit the gas. When he pulled out, he nicked the car parked in front of them and heard her cuss under her breath. He watched the men chase after them on foot and smiled as he hit the gas and left them in the dark street.

"Sorry, princess. I hope your insurance is paid up." He took the corner quickly and headed towards the highway, glancing in the rearview mirror to make sure they weren't being followed. "So, tell me where my brother is hanging his hat nowadays."

She glared over at him and crossed her arms over her chest.

"I know you may not have thought of this, but now you have a very pissed off drug lord after you as well."

She turned and looked at him. "Me? I didn't do anything?"

"Oh?" he said, smiling. "Do you think they didn't grab the plates off this car?" He laughed. "Actually, they probably own the club we were in tonight. If you've been in there before or used your credit card to buy drinks, they'll know who you are within the next few hours."

He could tell she was thinking about it. "What do we do? Go to the police?"

He glanced in the rearview mirror again. "Where is my brother?"

She looked at him and frowned. "Fairplay."

He glanced at her and thought. Fairplay. His cousins' ranch. It could work. He had to make a few calls first, but so far he didn't think that Dante's men knew his real identity. The police chief was going to be pissed that he'd blown it, but at least they already had another man working on the inside who hadn't had his cover blown by the tall, dark-haired woman with the long sexy legs who sat next to him.

He turned his eyes back to the road and mentally shut off his libido.

BREAKING TRAVIS

DIGITAL ISBN: 978-1-942896-52-4

PRINT ISBN: 978-1-942896-53-1

Copyeditor: Erica Ellis – inkdeepediting.com

Missy's Moment

Breaking Travis

Roping Ryan

Wild Bride

Corey's Catch

Tessa's Turn

The Grayton Series

Last Resort

Someday Beach

Rip Current

In Too Deep

Swept Away

High Tide

Lucky Series

Unlucky In Love

Sweet Resolve

Best of Luck

A Little Luck

Silver Cove Series

Silver Lining

French Kiss

Happy Accident

Hidden Charm

A Silver Cove Christmas

Entangled Series – Paranormal Romance

The Awakening

The Beckoning

The Ascension

Haven, Montana Series

Closer to You

Never Let Go

Holding On

Pride Oregon Series

A Dash of Love

My Kind of Love

Season of Love

Tis the Season

Dare to Love

Where I Belong

Wildflowers Series

Summer Nights

Summer Heat

Stand Alone Books

Twisted Rock

For a complete list of books:

http://JillSanders.com

Jill Sanders is a New York Times, USA Today, and international bestselling author of Sweet Contemporary Romance, Romantic Suspense, Western Romance, and Paranormal Romance novels. With over 55 books in eleven series, translations into several different languages, and audiobooks there's plenty to choose from. Look for Jill's bestselling stories wherever romance books are sold or visit her at jillsanders.com

Jill comes from a large family with six siblings, including an identical twin. She was raised in the Pacific Northwest and later relocated to Colorado for college and a successful IT career before discovering her talent for writing sweet and sexy page-turners. After Colorado, she decided to move south, living in Texas and now making her home along the Emerald Coast of Florida. You will find that the settings of several of her series are inspired by her time spent living in these areas. She has two sons and off-set the testosterone in her house by adopting three furry little ladies that provide her company while she's locked in her writing cave. She enjoys heading to the beach, hiking, swimming, wine-tasting, and pickleball with her husband, and of course writing. If you have read any of her books, you may also notice that there is a love of food, especially sweets! She has been blamed for a few added pounds by her assistant, editor, and fans… donuts or pie anyone?

facebook.com/JillSandersBooks

twitter.com/JillMSanders

bookbub.com/authors/jill-sanders